HEARTS IN PERIL™

Terror on the Trail

Virginia Vaughan

Annie's®
AnniesFiction.com

Books in the Hearts in Peril series

Library of Congress-in-Publication Data
Terror on the Trail / by Virginia Vaughan
p. cm.
ISBN: 978-1-64025-795-5
I. Title
                    2023934915

AnniesFiction.com
(800) 282-6643
Hearts in Peril™
Series Creator: Shari Lohner
Series Editor: Amy Woods

10 11 12 13 14 | Printed in China | 9 8 7 6 5 4 3 2 1

*N*atchez Trace Parkway Ranger Tory Mills had responded to plenty of calls in her ten years as a law enforcement ranger for the National Park Service, but receiving a call about a possible homicide gave her pause. While it happened occasionally—just like everywhere else—murder wasn't a frequent occurrence on the Trace.

She accepted the call from dispatch, then turned her National Park Services SUV down the two-lane road toward the mile marker from where the call had originated. There was no commercial traffic allowed on the 444-mile parkway that ran from Natchez, Mississippi, all the way to Nashville, Tennessee. Cell service was spotty along the Trace, as it was all national forestland. Though the caller had gotten through, that didn't guarantee Tory would have service too. She checked to make sure her radio was charged. She would need it.

She pulled into a roundabout with a small parking lot and a marker that declared a historical figure had once stopped there. The Trace was full of such markers, where travelers liked to stop, stretch their legs, and learn a little bit about the area's history. The Trace was also a wonderful area for hiking, with abundant forests and trails. Tory spotted two empty vehicles and assumed that was what their occupants had been doing.

A young woman sporting hiking gear and a ponytail met her at the base of the tree line, where she could see a small trail blazed through the woods. "Ranger, over here. The body is this way."

Tory grabbed her bag of supplies from the back of her SUV, then followed the hiker up the narrow path. After about a quarter of a mile, the path opened into a clearing. The woman who'd been her guide hurried over to a man who was obviously a companion. Another man—older than the other two visitors, probably in his late forties—stood to the side.

But it was the body on the ground that caught and held Tory's attention.

Tory set down her bag, then went to examine the situation.

Female. Late teens to early twenties. Her head was hidden by the tree next to her, but the rest of her body was in plain sight. Her hands were bound behind her with duct tape. Oddly, a red tube sock was wrapped around the deceased woman's neck, which Tory surmised had probably been the instrument used to strangle her, should the coroner conclude that strangulation was in fact the cause of death.

Tory stopped herself from going down that line of thinking. That wasn't her job. Her job was to secure the scene and call in the forensics team and the Investigative Services Branch. The ISB would handle the investigation. The Natchez Trace fell under the jurisdiction of the National Park Service, and the ISB handled all their major criminal cases.

She faced the group. One of them must have made the 911 call that had brought Tory to the scene. "I'm Ranger Mills. Can one of you tell me what happened here?"

"I found her," the older man stated as he stepped forward. "I was hiking the trail and came upon her lying there. My name is Alton Banks." He handed Tory a photo ID, and she used her phone to snap a picture of it. She would print off the photo back at the office, then place it in the file she passed along to the ISB.

Tory recognized Mr. Banks. She'd seen him several times up and down the Trace and even in town over the past week. He seemed to be a regular hiker.

Natchez had been a thriving community in the 1700s and 1800s, when it was a port town for shipping goods down the Mississippi River. Before the Civil War, it was home to more millionaires than any other city in the US, and many of the antebellum mansions had since been restored and preserved. Stepping into the city of Natchez was like taking a stroll back in time, and the Natchez Trace Parkway commemorated the trail that traders had taken to return North after floating their goods downriver.

Tory had lived in Natchez all her life. She'd grown up there and loved the history, the traditions, and especially the nature preserves.

She hated to see her beloved Natchez Trace marred by murder.

With limited cell phone service on the Trace, she took out her radio and contacted the ranger station.

"Tory, what did you find?" Her boss, Supervisory Ranger Christopher Moore, had forwarded the 911 call to her.

"It's like the caller stated—there's a body. Young. Female."

"Any chance this was a natural death or an accident?" her boss asked.

She'd worked with him long enough to recognize the hopeful anticipation in his voice.

Tory took in the woman lying on the ground. "Probably not. You'd better call in the ISB. I'll cordon off the area until they arrive."

She ended the call, then surveyed the scene. It was unlikely that any other humans would trample through the clearing, but wildlife was a concern.

The woman from the couple stepped forward. "Can we give our statements and go? We've already lost a lot of daylight for hiking."

Tory hated to waste their time. They'd done the right thing in calling in the authorities, but leaving wasn't an option for the time being. "I'm sorry, but no. You'll need to stay and give your statement to the ISB agents when they arrive."

"And how long will that be?" the woman asked, an impatient edge to her tone.

The Investigative Services Branch would have to fly in from either the district office in Atlanta or wherever else they happened to be working on another case.

"I can't say exactly, but it'll probably be a while."

The woman's companion grunted and ran a frustrated hand through his hair. "I told you we shouldn't have stayed."

"It was the right thing to do," the woman insisted, although Tory noticed she didn't appear as certain as she might have been earlier.

Tory cleared her throat. "Let me secure the scene, then I'll take your preliminary statements. If the ISB agent is delayed, perhaps I can arrange something."

It was the best she could offer. She couldn't allow them to leave, especially before eliminating the possibility that they were somehow involved in the victim's demise. She checked her watch before grabbing the crime scene tape and roping off the area surrounding the body. Hopefully, members of the Adams County Sheriff's Office would arrive soon to back her up and process the scene. The National Park Service had no forensics capabilities and often relied on local and state resources like the sheriff's office, the Natchez Police Department, and the state crime lab.

After securing the scene, Tory turned her attention back to the witnesses. "Thank you all for your patience. I'm certain the investigator from the ISB will have questions about what happened here today, but for now, I'd like to take preliminary statements while the information is still fresh in your minds." She took out a notebook and pen to jot down their responses.

Tory addressed the older man first. He was tan and fit, obviously a seasoned hiker. "I've seen you around the area over the last few weeks." She already had a photo of his license and opened her phone to read the name again. "Alton Banks? What were you doing here, Mr. Banks?"

"I'm in town to hike the Trace and see the sights. Got my camper parked over at the Pebble Springs Campground."

She knew the area well. "You said you found the body?"

He nodded. "I had my cell phone with me, and thankfully I had enough signal to call 911."

"Did you move the body at all?" Tory asked, carefully studying his features.

"Absolutely not. It was obvious she was dead, so I didn't touch the body. I waited here until you arrived. These two showed up a few minutes later."

Alton pointed a thumb toward the couple, who stood a few feet away. They both appeared to be in their midtwenties and were dressed in hiking gear.

"Thank you, Mr. Banks." Tory moved on toward the couple. "What are your names?"

"Jake and Shelia Hall." The man produced his wallet and handed over his identification, his wife following suit.

Tory used her cell phone to snap photos of both ID cards before returning them. "How did you wind up here?"

The woman answered. "We came upon the scene and found Mr. Banks here, but we thought we should hang around until the police arrived because of what we saw."

"And what was that?"

"A man running toward his truck at the base of the trail," Jake explained. "We had parked and were getting ready to hike when he darted out from the woods. He ran right into Shelia and didn't even stop to apologize. He hopped into a white pickup and drove away."

"Can you describe him?"

"Tall, probably about the same height as Jake," Shelia said. "A little over six feet. Dark hair. Maybe thirty to forty years old."

"Did you happen to get a plate number for the truck?"

They shook their heads with clear regret.

"We're sorry," Shelia added. "We thought he was simply in a hurry. We had no idea it might be for such an awful reason as this."

Tory understood, as she also understood their anxiety to leave. They'd ventured out to hike the many trails the Trace had to offer, and daylight was precious. But a woman was dead, likely murdered, and their eyewitness accounts could help catch the person responsible. Tory was going to do everything in her power to help the ISB agent assigned to the case. She pulled out her radio and called in the information about the man seen potentially fleeing the scene, and instructed dispatch to issue a BOLO—or Be on the Lookout—for anyone matching the vehicle or suspect's description.

Movement in the brush caught Tory's attention, and she tensed until she spotted the familiar ranger uniform and saw her boss enter the clearing. It wasn't often that he followed up on a scene, but murder wasn't a common occurrence.

"Chris, you made it."

He took off his hat and wiped sweat from his brow. "Sheriff's deputies are right behind me." He walked over to see the body and shook his head in dismay. "I've received word from the ISB that someone is on their way into town now. They're classifying this case as a top priority."

She wasn't surprised, even though she knew they stayed busy. With fewer than forty agents on the ISB team and over four hundred sites to cover, they were stretched thin, but murder would have to take a front seat to other, lesser crimes.

"They don't want us to remove the body until the agent arrives," Chris added.

She surveyed the scene. "The coroner isn't here yet, so we have a bit of time, but I'm not sure we have the jurisdiction to tell him whether he can move the body."

Besides that, the brutal August heat was bearing down hard.

"You're right," Chris said. "And Mason doesn't like to be told what to do."

She grimaced. The Adams County coroner, Don Mason, was known for doing things his way and resenting any interference, real or perceived. He liked to do his job efficiently and well, which was a good thing, but Tory didn't relish having to convince him to stay until the ISB agent arrived.

The forensic team from the Adams County Sheriff's Office joined Tory and Chris and promptly assembled a tent over the scene, in order to preserve evidence against the heat.

It was nearly two hours before Mason arrived. Tory found herself hoping that, by the time the coroner finished his examination and ordered the body removed, the ISB agent would have arrived. But by hour three, the witnesses were overheated and impatient to leave. They'd repeated their statements to the Natchez sheriff's deputies and complained further about having to remain.

Normally, Tory would release them, but since the ISB agent was en route, she decided to have them stay. They weren't happy about it, but she wasn't in the job to make friends. In an effort to keep them as comfortable as possible, she offered each a bottle of water from the cooler in her SUV. They'd probably finished whatever water they'd brought for hiking hours before. The couple accepted the water, but Mr. Banks waved it off. He seemed intent on watching the forensics team as they photographed the crime scene and collected evidence.

One of the deputies approached Tory. "Mason has sent for a gurney to transport the body. He's ready to go. Your ISB agent's time is up."

For at least the millionth time, Tory wished she had an estimated time of arrival on the still-absent ISB agent. Without one, she would have to wing it.

She rushed toward the coroner. "The ISB agent has specifically asked that we keep the body here until she arrives. She's on her way now."

Mason glared at her. "I work for the county, Ranger Mills. I don't answer to the ISB. It's hot out, and I prefer to get this victim back to my office before any evidence is compromised even more than it already has been. The ISB agent can come to my office once she arrives, or better yet, read my report."

Tory was about to protest again when Chris joined them. "I got the call on my radio. They're here."

Relief filled her. "The ISB agent?"

"Not exactly. It's the FBI."

It wasn't unusual for the FBI to take over or assist on cases when the ISB was overwhelmed, so it wasn't much of a surprise to hear they'd sent an FBI agent instead.

It wasn't much of a surprise—until the brush cleared and she spotted the agent in question.

Her pulse pounded in her ears as a familiar figure made his way into the clearing.

His broad shoulders had filled out even more against his suit coat, and his familiar brown eyes sparkled when he removed his sunglasses.

Tory's breath caught in her throat, and all the people and commotion that had suddenly invaded her crime scene faded into the background, as the man she'd once loved strolled back into her life.

Matt Shepherd, FBI agent extraordinaire, had finally come home after fifteen years away.

And it had taken a dead body to bring him back.

$\mathcal{M}$att stepped into the clearing and watched as Tory's eyes widened.

He wasn't as surprised to see her as she was to see him. He'd gotten word on the plane ride from Great Smoky Mountains National Park that she'd been the responding ranger on duty. He probably should have given her a heads-up that he was taking over the case, but he hadn't been sure how to do that without making everything about their shared past instead of the homicide victim.

Still, he couldn't help but appreciate the way Tory's dark lashes still framed her lovely green eyes, surprised as her expression was. Even on a hot August afternoon in Mississippi, with her long, dark hair in a neat ponytail and her ranger uniform damp with perspiration, she was beautiful. And she'd grown even more so than the last time he'd seen her, all those years ago when he'd left to join the FBI.

But he dragged his thoughts away from her and back to the case. They were both professionals, and he wasn't in town for a reunion with his childhood sweetheart. "Hello, Tory."

"Matt, what are you doing here?"

The details of the case had piqued his attention while he'd been working a similar homicide in the Smokies with ISB Agent Vivian Ferguson. "I'm working with the ISB on this case. Can you give me a brief overview of what you've found?"

Tory contained her shock and pulled out her notebook. "A witness found a woman's body and called 911. I cordoned off the scene and took preliminary witness statements. A couple claims to have seen a man fleeing the scene. They gave a description of the man and his vehicle, and a BOLO has been issued. The county forensics team is here to process the scene and gather evidence, along with the coroner, who is ready to transport the body back to the morgue."

Matt spotted the coroner's team readying the body and hurried past Tory. "Excuse me, please." He showed his FBI credentials to an older, gruff-looking man with what appeared to be a permanent scowl, who wore protective gloves, booties, and a mask. "Can I have a moment to survey the scene before you remove the victim, please, Mr. . . . ?"

"Mason. I'm the county coroner."

"Mr. Mason, I appreciate that you're busy. I promise I won't keep you long," Matt told him. He saw the irritation on the man's face, but it wasn't often he got the chance to examine a crime scene so early in an investigation. He wasn't going to allow a little inconvenience to stop him.

The coroner glanced at his watch, then reluctantly moved aside and instructed his staff to do so as well. Matt wasn't sure if it was his FBI credentials, or if Mason wasn't as sour as he appeared, but he was thankful for their action. Usually, all he saw were crime scene photos and forensic reports days after the fact. A firsthand examination of the body and scene could prove helpful.

It was the first time he'd been so close to seeing a victim after they'd been found—and so close to where he knew the killer had been mere hours before.

He carefully went over the scene, mentally noting details. The victim was young and female, with a red tube sock tied around her neck, and her body had been discovered in a national park site. He rubbed his chin as the weight of the sight hit him.

It seemed the serial killer he'd been chasing for months had moved to Natchez.

Matt would have to wait on the coroner's opinion, officially, but based on his experience, the victim had likely been dead for a few hours, and it had taken Matt less than three to arrive in town.

His early arrival could be the advantage he needed to finally capture the killer and get justice for the victims.

He stood and gestured to the team, indicating that it was okay to move the body. "Thank you." He turned to Tory. "Have you gotten photos and measurements?"

"The county forensics team collected evidence from the scene and from the body. I made sure photographs were taken from all angles. I also kept the witnesses on-site when I heard ISB was en route."

Matt peered toward a group of civilians at the edge of the crime scene. They appeared sweaty and irritated, and he couldn't blame them. He'd only been out of his air-conditioned SUV for a few minutes, but the Mississippi summer heat had smacked him hard when he'd gotten off the plane. He was anxious to shed his suit jacket. He'd forgotten how stifling the summer climate could be in Natchez, especially after experiencing the cooler mountain air of the Great Smoky Mountains.

He pulled out his credentials as he approached the group. "I'm Special Agent Matt Shepherd with the FBI. I'd like you all to repeat what you've told other law enforcement today."

The older man stepped forward. "I found her. I was out for a hike when I came across her body lying on the ground."

"And your name is?"

"Alton Banks. I gave the ranger all my information when she first arrived."

"That's good, Mr. Banks, and I appreciate your patience. Were you alone when you discovered the victim?"

"Yes, I was hiking the trail on my own."

"Did you see anyone around?"

"No, I didn't see anyone until these two came upon the scene." He indicated the other man and woman.

Matt questioned the couple as well, and they told him about the man they'd seen fleeing the scene. Generally, Matt had to depend on first responders' notes, interviewing witnesses himself several days or longer after the crime. It was a new and enlightening experience to be able to speak with them while the incident was fresh in their minds.

"Can we go now?" the woman demanded, arms crossed as she tapped a foot against the dirt.

"Did Ranger Mills take down your contact information?"

They confirmed that she had, so he dismissed them. "Then you're free to go. Thank you for your assistance. We'll contact you if we require more information."

As the witnesses left, Matt found Tory standing behind him. He could have sworn he saw steam coming out of her ears. "I have to say, Matt, I'm not thrilled that you're coming in after me and repeating the work I've already done."

"That's not my aim here, Tory. I have to make certain everything about this case is airtight. We can't have any missteps."

She put her hand on her hip, and even after nearly fifteen years apart, he recognized the irritation in her stance. "What are you even doing here, Matt?"

Her tone indicated she was more interested in the fact that he was treading on her turf than in why he'd been assigned to the case.

"I'm partnering with ISB Agent Vivian Ferguson on this case. I was with her when the call came in. She stayed behind to finish work at another crime scene, so I came in her stead."

Tory squinted at him in the glaring sun. "What was the rush? I've never seen ISB or the FBI show up this quickly, even for a murder case."

He hesitated before speaking. "It might be connected to another case we're investigating. Agent Ferguson sent me to verify."

"What's the other case?" Tory pressed.

"I'll explain back at the ranger station. I'm establishing a task force between the FBI, National Park Services, Natchez PD, and the sheriff's office. I want to start working this case hard, right away. We need to put a rush on everything."

Her eyes widened as she realized the seriousness of the situation. "It's terrible that a murder has occurred, but is there a reason for the added urgency?"

"Yes." Matt wasn't ready to go public with the possibility that a serial killer might be lurking in the area. He had to verify the evidence first before making that determination, although his gut told him it was true. He didn't want it to leak to the papers and cause unnecessary alarm.

Mostly, Matt didn't want to scare off the killer. Not when he was so close.

But the touch of concern on Tory's face moved him. Someone should know what was happening, and he trusted her. He took a step closer to her and lowered his voice. "It could be a serial case."

She stiffened at the notion. "I'll finish up here and meet you back at the ranger station."

Matt hopped back into the black SUV that had been waiting for him at the airport when he'd landed. He headed for the ranger station, which he knew was several more miles up the Trace. His pulse was still rapid after seeing Tory again. He'd thought he'd been prepared for it, but the shock was surprising.

Her dark hair had been pulled back into a ponytail, but he recalled how she used to wear it down in soft curls that framed her face. Her wide green eyes and easy smile. He hadn't expected to be so shaken by their reunion.

He'd told himself it was simply another assignment, and that seeing her again wouldn't matter.

How wrong he'd been.

And not merely from a personal standpoint. He was impressed with her attention to detail at the crime scene. Every box had been checked and every detail accounted for. Nothing had gotten past her. He'd worked with far less impressive local law enforcement before.

He clicked on Vivian's name in his contact list and waited for the call to connect.

"Agent Ferguson," she answered.

"It's Matt. I'm in Natchez. I just left the crime scene."

"And?"

He heard the unspoken question in her tone—was it what they'd suspected, after hearing the details?

"This crime scene was nearly identical to the others we've investigated, right down to the red tube sock tied around the victim's neck."

He and Vivian had studied multiple crime scenes with similar traits to the one he'd observed, convincing him that a serial killer was indeed on the loose. From what Matt and Vivian had gleaned so far, he—statistically, serial killers were primarily male—killed his victim, tied a sock around her neck, then dumped her body in a national park. So far, six victims in two different national parks had been identified and it seemed the murderer was getting started in Natchez.

"I'll have to wait for the official cause of death," Matt continued, "but I believe it's our guy."

He heard Vivian pause on the other end of the line. "I have some follow-up to take care of here, but then I'll head to Natchez as soon as I can."

Prior to his flight, Matt and Vivian had been working the latest crime scene in Great Smoky Mountains National Park. So far, they had found three women murdered and dumped in the same park, all nearly identical to the Natchez crime scene. "I'll put a team together and get to work here."

"I don't have to tell you that we're up against the clock."

Matt knew that as well as she did. They had to get as much information as possible about the killer before he took another life.

Arriving at the ranger station, Matt parked the SUV. The local sheriff and the Natchez chief of police were both there, along with the supervisory ranger. He introduced himself to each officer.

"I'm Supervisory Ranger Chris Moore." Chris was a fortyish, clean-cut man with a firm handshake. He struck Matt right away as a by-the-book sort of supervisor. If Chris was the one who'd trained Tory, Matt was impressed.

Next, a burly, bald guy stuck out a hand. "Bruce Scott, Chief of Natchez Police Department."

The third officer, tall and tan, stood. "Sheriff John Ford, Adams County."

"It's nice to meet you all," Matt said, meaning it. "I'd like you to make the case I'm about to discuss a top priority."

Bruce folded his arms. "What is it?"

"I've been working with ISB on a string of murders that appear to have been committed by the same person. Though we're not positive that the killer is a male, statistics speak to that likelihood. He seems to kill in threes, strangling his victims, then tying a red tube sock around their necks before dumping their bodies in a national park. After the third victim, he moves on to the next park. This is our third park, and we've had six previous victims so far."

"And you're certain this victim is another of his?" Moore asked.

"Not until I have more evidence, but it fits the pattern. And if it is our guy, he's just getting started."

Moore's jaw clenched. "A serial killer loose on the Trace."

"And in our town," Chief Scott added. "You said he dumps his victims on park land. Are they abducted and killed there as well?"

Matt shook his head. "We believe he abducts and kills them elsewhere, then leaves them to be found in the parks. So far, we haven't found any blood spatter or trace evidence to suggest any of the victims were killed where they were left."

"So this nightmare belongs to all of us," the sheriff concluded.

"Yes sir, it does. I want to establish a task force to work this case as efficiently as possible. I'll have to set up a command post. I'm hoping we can uncover the killer's identity before he claims his second victim on the Natchez Trace."

It was imperative that they capture the culprit before the third victim. After that, according to his established pattern, he would leave for another location, and they would be stuck starting over from scratch, waiting for him to kill again.

"We'll do whatever we can to help," Ranger Moore stated.

"Our office is in downtown Natchez," Sheriff Ford added. "We can offer you a conference room to operate from."

"Thank you. That'll work," Matt agreed. "I'd also appreciate personnel assigned to my team from each of you."

"No problem."

The sheriff and chief each shook Matt's hand before leaving, presumably to select said personnel.

Matt stayed behind to speak with Ranger Moore. "Agent Ferguson of the ISB has been delayed. I'd like to work closely with the rangers on this case."

"We're happy to help, but we're a small station. I have eight rangers in total," Moore explained.

"I was impressed with Ranger Mills today," Matt said. "She did good work. I'd like her to be part of my task force if you can spare her."

Moore nodded. "I'll make sure she's available."

Matt thanked the ranger and exited his office, nearly running into Tory on her way in.

She flashed him a smirk. "I see you're making yourself at home."

Ranger Moore appeared in his office doorway. "Tory, can I see you for a moment?"

She followed her boss into the small room. She wasn't going to be happy when Moore relayed the information that she'd been recruited to help Matt.

But her feelings couldn't be his main concern. She was smart, capable, and familiar with the area. He'd grown up in Natchez, but he'd been away for a long time. No one knew Natchez or the Trace like Tory Mills.

Matt needed her on his side.

$\mathcal{T}$ory's anxiety level increased with every word as Chris explained her new assignment.

Seeing Matt again after fifteen years was surreal. They'd been high school sweethearts and planned to get married, but a job offer with the FBI had prompted him to leave for Quantico instead after graduation. She'd kept up with his career and, as her heart began to heal after being left behind, came to see that the FBI had been the right choice for him. He'd become successful and was at the top of his career. She was happy for him—really.

But working with him? That would be beyond awkward.

"You have to assign this task to someone else, Chris." She swallowed hard, trying to figure out how to convey the truth without going too in depth. "Matt and I have history. It's complicated."

"I'm sorry, Tory. He asked for you specifically." He stood and walked around the desk to where she sat. "Besides, I think this is a good move for you. Working with the FBI on a serial case. It'll help when you apply for a position with the ISB."

Chris had been on her case about applying for a position with ISB, but she wasn't sure it was what she wanted. It would entail moving, and she loved Natchez. She'd been born and raised there and loved everything about living in such a historic town. She was also happily settled in a little cabin not far from the Trace and had a job she loved.

She hadn't been willing to leave her hometown to further Matt's career. Would she want to leave it to further her own?

"Listen," Chris said, "whatever happened between you and this fed, you're both professionals with a job to do. I'm sure you can get past it and work together for a little while. Besides, how many opportunities do you get to investigate a possible serial killer? You can't let this opportunity pass you by, Tory. I won't allow it."

She gritted her teeth. Why was Chris so insistent that she move up the ladder? She couldn't deny that working a serial killer case intrigued her, but being around Matt Shepherd again was the last thing she wanted.

He'd landed in town a few hours before. How had he managed to flip her life upside down already?

She left Chris's office and spotted Matt outside, standing next to his black SUV. Chris had said that Matt specifically requested her for his team, which seemed odd to her given their history. She would have assumed Matt was as anxious to avoid her as she was him. He must have had a reason to feel otherwise.

She decided to find out what that reason was, and pushed through the door to the parking lot before she could change her mind. Her feet crunched against the gravel as she approached him. "Why me, Matt?"

He didn't even bother to raise his head from a notepad he was reading. "Pardon?"

"Why did you request that I assist you with this investigation?" she asked. "There are other rangers and, given our past, I think it might be a good idea to tap someone else for this job."

He took off his sunglasses and locked eyes with her, his sharp hazel gaze piercing her as it always had. She fought the urge to squirm.

"You're worried it will be awkward?" he asked.

Of course it would be awkward. One minute they'd been madly in love. The next he was gone from her life to follow his dream to work for the FBI—a dream that evidently did not include her.

"What if I give you my word that this has nothing to do with that?

It's pure business, Tory. You're more familiar with Natchez than anyone, so you're the best person to help me catch this killer."

"That's silly, Matt. You grew up here."

"But I haven't set foot here in fifteen years. You've had your ear to the ground all this time. You're a ranger now, which means you've got the training and skills to handle this case. Plus, you're smart and detail oriented. You would have proven that today even if I hadn't already known it. Whenever I work with local law enforcement, I always want someone who's an expert in the area." He took a deep breath. "I need you on this case, Tory. You're the best chance we have at stopping this guy and saving countless lives."

Serial killers were always terrible, but the way his jaw tensed and his shoulders flexed told her that his case must be particularly bad. Her mind flashed back to the young woman she'd found earlier that day. Tory had done her best to compartmentalize the evil act in order to do her job, but the truth of the matter hit her. A precious young life had been taken. Someone out there was preying on women in her town. Her stomach rolled at the thought.

And if Matt meant what he said, and it truly was pure business—well, maybe she could work with that.

"Okay, I'll do it."

"Thank you." He pulled a briefcase from the back seat of the SUV, and opened it on the hood of the vehicle, revealing some photographs. "The man we're searching for has already murdered six women. Today's victim makes number seven. He kills three women, takes a piece of jewelry from them as a souvenir—according to several victims' family members—then dumps their bodies on national park land. We've already discovered victims in Glacier National Park, Great Smoky Mountains, and now here. After the third victim in each park, he moves on to a different national park area. It's his pattern."

She took the photographs and flipped through the other victims as Matt's meaning grew clearer. "He's getting started here in Natchez."

"Yes, but he's here, and so are we. For the first time, we're not behind him. Our job is to capture him before he completes this cycle and moves on."

She stared at the crime scene photos. Six women—seven including the current victim—all murdered and dumped at the offender's whim.

Tory sighed. Matt was right. Everything about the victim they'd discovered today matched the other crime scenes, down to the red tube sock wrapped around her neck.

Raising her chin, she peered up into his handsome familiar face. She'd loved him once upon a time. She'd even planned on marrying him, but circumstances had changed. Fifteen years was a long time ago. They were different people, and a man she hardly knew anymore was asking her to help him stop a killer in the hometown she loved.

Tory handed back the crime scene photos. "What's our next move?"

4

$\mathcal{M}$att was grateful to have Tory on his team. He was certain they could keep things from getting awkward between them. After all, their relationship had ended fifteen years before. He'd left for the FBI academy, and she'd made the choice to remain in Natchez. Surely they could keep their interactions strictly professional.

But if that were the case, then why had his heart skipped a beat the moment he'd gazed into her beautiful green eyes?

The team set up shop in a conference room at the sheriff's office, and he arranged his laptop and evidence boards, pinning the latest victim's photograph in the center. Their first assignment was to identify the young woman. He also added photographs of the other six victims as a reminder to himself and anyone working on the task force that there was a bigger picture. They were hunting a serial killer who was clearly far from finished, which upped the stakes even more. Matt grouped the three victims they'd uncovered from Glacier National Park together, then did the same with the three victims from Great Smoky Mountains National Park. If they were fortunate, they wouldn't have to add another one for Natchez.

The age of the victims ranged from eighteen to thirty-three. The women had hardly any of the usual shared traits—such as body type, pre-abduction behavior, or profession—though the victims all had blonde or light-colored hair. There were no brunette victims so far, which could indicate a pattern. Additionally, there were similarities in the way they had been killed—the cause of death being manual strangulation, the inclusion of a red tube sock, and the way their hands were bound behind their backs with duct tape before the bodies had been dumped. Most notable was the fact that all seven victims had been placed in areas that saw considerable traffic, the most recent in a clearing on a well-traveled hiking trail. The killer wasn't hiding his victims. He wanted law enforcement to be aware that he was out there.

As requested, Matt had several local deputies and Natchez police officers at his disposal, as well as Tory's assistance. He set them to identifying their latest victim and canvassing for other possible witnesses to the crime.

Tory knocked on the conference room door, then opened it and entered without waiting for a response. "Here are the background checks on our witnesses today."

It sometimes struck people as odd that law enforcement would run background checks on witnesses, but they had to know everyone providing information was on the up and up.

"Anything suspicious?" he asked.

She didn't answer immediately, and he looked up to see her staring at his evidence board. It was shocking to see the full scope of the killer's viciousness for the first time.

"Tory?" he asked, keeping his tone gentle. "Did any of the witnesses have priors?"

She shook her head and did her best to turn her attention back to the question at hand. "Mr. Banks has a speeding ticket on his file, but nothing major. The Halls both have clean records."

He glanced over the file she'd handed him, which contained all three witnesses' driver's licenses and background information. Everything seemed to be in order.

Good. The quicker they could eliminate red flags, the sooner they could move on.

Matt straightened in his chair, trying to focus on the case despite his sudden awareness of the scent of Tory's shampoo, an enchanting combination of lavender and vanilla.

She folded her arms and walked over to the evidence board. A frown creased her features as she read the details of each victim. "How long have you been chasing this guy?"

Matt joined her. "About a year and a half. The first victim was Karen Fields, a thirty-three-year-old wife and mother." He pointed to a photograph of Fields under the Glacier National Park group. "At first, the rangers thought she must have gotten separated from a group and come upon a predator, but her family claimed she didn't enjoy hiking. They couldn't even recall the last time she'd been to the national park. Then, a week later, Jada Fontenot was found murdered and posed almost exactly the same way, in a different spot, but still on Glacier land." He pointed to Fontenot's picture. "By that time, ISB had been called in and had gotten the autopsy report back on Karen Fields, which indicated that she'd been manually strangled."

Tory stared at him, her eyes wide. "Manually strangled? He didn't use the tube sock to strangle them?"

Matt shook his head. That detail had struck him as well. "We don't have any idea yet why the killer adds the sock, but we've found no evidence that he uses it as part of his murder methodology. It must hold some significance to him, but it's definitely become part of his modus operandi, whatever the reason."

"Maybe it's his calling card, to tell law enforcement that it's his work."

Matt folded his arms, appreciating the fact that they were on the same page. "I've profiled this killer as someone who is attention-seeking. Like you said, I think he's making it clear to us which victims he killed, and he doesn't believe that the police, ISB, or FBI are smart enough to uncover his identity."

"How do you figure that?"

"He's not hiding these victims, Tory. He's dumping them right out there in plain sight, which means he wants them to be found and is willing to risk getting caught. Based on the organization and details of each scene, I've also profiled the murderer as being very meticulous. There's not a lot of evidence left behind. He doesn't want us to see where the victims were abducted or actually killed. There's no obvious blood or other evidence at the sites where they're disposed of, which tells me he's killing them elsewhere and posing their bodies in a location that ensures they're found. He's letting us see what he wants us to see. That behavior suggests a need for control."

She was watching him with a hint of amazement in her expression. "What else can you tell me about him?"

"He's probably a white male. Thirty to fifty-five years old. As I said, he leaves behind very little evidence except what he wants us to see, which tells me he's meticulous and organized. There are no signs of hesitation, so he's experienced and has probably been killing for years. For that reason, I'd place him higher up on the age scale, maybe in his fifties." After so many months, he knew the profile by heart, but it helped him to go over the information again, especially with fresh eyes like Tory's.

She watched him without interruption, her expression calculating. He could tell that she was likely committing the information to memory.

"I think there may be previous victims who haven't been attributed to him, and that may make him feel invisible, unappreciated. It may also mean he's changed his methods over time to make certain his most recent victims are discovered. Hence the red tube socks and national park dumping sites. I've got a team back at the Bureau searching for other victims that match his signature, but with no way of knowing where he originated from, it won't be easy. That's why it's so important we find him while he's sticking to this new pattern. These murders vary by day of the week, times of day, even season of the year, which tells me he's probably not tied to a nine-to-five job unless he has a lot of vacation time or runs his own business. He has the ability to travel from park to park, so he's mobile. He probably has an occupation that allows him freedom to travel, but given my speculation about his age, it's also possible he's traveling with family. There are groups of retirees who wander around the country in RVs. It's quite the community, so I'm considering that a possibility too. He would appear controlling to the people around him, and he enjoys being the one in charge because, again, he thinks he's smarter than anyone else in the room." He stopped talking and took a deep breath.

"Wow, that's impressive," Tory said. "You got all of that from going over crime scenes? You should be an FBI profiler."

Matt shrugged. "I considered going that route, but they don't get to work out in the field very often, and I enjoy the hands-on aspect of my job. But it's not all profiling technique, Tory." He swallowed as a chill went up his spine. He could trust her with anything, but that didn't make what he was about to share any easier to stomach. "The killer has reached out to me. He's sent letters. He's dubbed himself the 'National Park Predator.' This choice to communicate directly with me reveals that he's getting bored, which tells me he is disappointed that no one has gotten close to identifying him yet. He's desperate for attention, which is probably why he's added the detail of the red tube sock—so there is no doubt it's him. I've seen a lot of things in my time with the FBI and have learned a lot about human behavior and psychology. It's imperative if we want to stop the worst of the worst from committing more atrocities."

Matt found it uncomfortable to open up to Tory about his time with the FBI. After all, his choice to accept the position had been the catalyst that eventually led to their painful breakup. He hadn't meant for things to happen that way, but he couldn't change the course their lives had taken. He'd been young when he'd landed the opportunity, and foolishly believed that she would take that journey with him when he left for the academy.

A deputy entered the room and handed Tory a slip of paper. She thanked him, and he left.

"What is it?" Matt asked.

"An update on the possible identity of our victim. Natchez Police Department received a call about a missing woman matching our victim's description. Twenty-year-old Liddy Martin. She works as a waitress at the Natchez Diner downtown. Her parents reported her missing when she didn't come home from work last night. Normally, they don't accept a missing person report so soon, but the officer who took the call knew the family and promised to check it out."

"Has her family been notified?"

Tory shook her head, her eyes filled with regret. "Not yet."

Talking with the families of deceased loved ones had never been his strong suit, but it had to be done. He needed a positive identification before gathering information about the victim and her actions in the hours before she died. He was rarely called on to carry out the difficult task, since families were usually notified by local law enforcement long before he entered an investigation, but everything about the case was different.

"I can handle it," Tory said.

"I'll come too. We'll have to question the family about what was going on in her life. I want to find out where she was abducted from and when."

Tory regarded him as he gathered his files.

"What?" he asked.

Tory hesitated. "Why don't you let me do the talking?" She reached out a hand, palm up. "These people are about to find out that they've lost their daughter. They're not going to be up for an interrogation."

He acquiesced to that request. Truthfully, he was glad to let her handle it. Dealing with strong emotions wasn't something he was particularly adept at. He was more accustomed to managing the facts of a case. While Tory had strength in spades, it was her kindness to others that had always been her best quality, and he was certain that hadn't changed. He'd never seen her act out in anger in any tough situation, including in high school when she'd caught a group of mean girls picking on a less popular student. Tory had de-escalated the tension calmly and efficiently so that the other student could get to safety, without further agitating the bullies. Her empathy for the victim's family was another reason he could tell they were going to work well together on the case.

Matt and Tory walked outside to where his SUV was parked on the street. They climbed inside, and he punched the address listed on Liddy Martin's driver's license into his GPS. The directions led them to a nice neighborhood of neat homes. They parked in front of a butter-yellow house with sky-blue shutters and a perfectly manicured lawn. Even from the outside, Matt could tell the family within it was happy, and he dreaded poisoning that happiness.

They trudged up the sidewalk, and Tory knocked on the door. A woman Matt guessed to be Mrs. Martin, Liddy's mother, opened it—and broke down at the sight of Tory's park ranger uniform and badge.

Mrs. Martin led them to a clean, comfortable living room, where they met Liddy's father and sister, Kara, who perched on the edges of their seats on the sofa, obviously hoping for a better outcome.

"Mr. and Mrs. Martin, I'm Ranger Tory Mills of the National Park Service," Tory said, her tone the perfect mixture of kindness and competence. "This is Special Agent Matt Shepherd with the FBI. May we speak to you for a moment?"

Mr. Martin put his arm around his wife as she sat next to him. "Is—is it Liddy?" he asked, his voice trembling. "Have you found her?"

"I'm afraid so," Tory answered as she and Matt took armchairs opposite the family. "A woman's body was found this morning on the Trace." She handed them a photograph from the coroner, showing the victim's face so that the family could make a formal identification. "Is this your daughter?"

They all burst into tears.

"Yes, that's her," Mr. Martin sobbed. "That's our Liddy."

"Who did this?" Liddy's mother asked. "Who did this to our baby?"

"We're investigating," Tory responded, putting the photograph away. Matt was in awe of both her composure and compassion. "I understand it will be difficult, but we need to ask you some questions. You reported Liddy missing late last night, correct?"

Mr. Martin cleared his throat, obviously trying to pull himself together. "Yes, she worked until midnight and she was always home by twelve thirty. We knew something was wrong when she wasn't home by two, and she wasn't answering our calls."

"When was the last time you spoke with her?"

"Yesterday afternoon before she left for work. She was fine. Everything was fine."

Matt leaned forward. "Did your daughter have any jewelry that she wore regularly?"

Kara answered that question. "Yes, she had a ring that belonged to our grandmother. Liddy always wore it. It had a ruby inside a silver heart." She stood to take a picture from a shelf and showed it to Tory and Matt, pointing out the ring visible on her sister's hand. "Here it is."

Matt jotted down the information. He didn't recall seeing that ring on the victim's body or in evidence, but he would double-check when he got the chance.

"Did you find it with her?" Kara asked.

He shook his head. "Not that I recall."

Kara fell back into her seat. "That means she could have been robbed. Someone killed my sister for a few bucks and my grandmother's ring?"

"We can't confirm that yet," Tory said. "We're still investigating the circumstances surrounding her death."

"What about any boyfriends?" Matt pressed forward. "Was she seeing anyone special? Or is there anyone who might have wanted to harm your daughter?"

"No," Mrs. Martin replied in a shaky voice. "Everybody liked Liddy. She was easy to get along with. Who would want to hurt her?"

"She broke up with her last boyfriend over a year ago," Kara told them. "She hadn't dated anyone since. She was attending classes at the community college and was really focused on getting her degree and becoming a teacher."

"Did she mention anyone who was bothering her, or causing her any grief?"

Mr. and Mrs. Martin shook their heads, but Kara burst into fresh tears. "Liddy was worried over the past few days. She mentioned that she thought someone was following her. She told me about it the other night but asked me not to say anything because she didn't want anyone to think she was silly and paranoid." Kara paused to wipe her eyes. "Was she right? Did she have a stalker? Should I have told, even though she asked me not to? Is this my fault?"

Tory raised an eyebrow at Matt, then turned her attention back to Liddy's sister. "Did she say who she thought might be following her? Did she know the person?"

Kara brushed another tear from her cheek. "She didn't tell me, but her coworkers at the diner might have seen or heard something."

"Thank you." Tory held Kara's gaze. "As for fault, that rests squarely on the shoulders of whoever chose to do this horrible thing to your sister. Don't let yourself believe anything else for so much as a second, okay?" Kara nodded tearfully, and Tory rose from her seat. "Thank you for speaking with us. Again, we are so very sorry for your loss."

Matt stood, but Liddy's sister grabbed his arm. "Promise me you'll find out who did this to her."

He'd promised himself he would find the killer, but he couldn't make such a vow to a victim's family member. "We'll do everything we can," he assured her. It would have to be enough.

Back in the SUV, Tory said, "We should go to the diner next and speak with her coworkers. If she was being stalked, does that change anything in the investigation?"

He considered the possibility. "It's important to be aware of, but no, it doesn't significantly change the investigation. A few of the other victims reported to family or friends that they felt they were being followed in the days before they were murdered."

"So these aren't crimes of opportunity?" Tory asked.

"Some never said a word about being followed. Perhaps they weren't, or maybe they simply didn't notice. Which means we don't have a conclusive pattern, unfortunately," he explained.

"What does your gut say?"

Normally, he tried to leave such things out of conversations with colleagues, but it was Tory. "I mentioned this before, but the killer seems to be a control freak. He wouldn't leave something like his victim's abduction up to chance."

She sat back in her seat, and he could sense that the case was getting to her. The awareness that there was a serial killer in her town must be upsetting, to say the least.

He drove downtown, where all kinds of shops and restaurants lined the streets. It was a popular spot with tourists, a stone's throw from the Mississippi River.

He parked on the street and got out, instantly hit with aromas that brought him back to his youth—the river, crawfish, and the blend of Cajun and Southern cooking.

They walked to the Natchez Diner, where Liddy Martin had worked and where she'd last been seen.

Matt asked to see the manager, Dwayne Hobbs, then broke the news about Liddy's death.

The older man paled as he slid into a chair. "I can't believe this is happening. She was here last night."

"What time did she leave?" Matt asked.

"It was a few minutes after midnight, right after we closed. She worked the last shift and we walked out together. She usually parked in the same place." Dwayne rubbed his face. "I should have offered to walk her to her car, but I was in a rush to get home. Besides, it's never been a problem before."

Matt made himself a note to check the manager's background for any suspicious behavior, but it was routine. He wanted to learn everything he could about the people in the victim's life—anyone could be a suspect.

"Did Liddy ever mention that she thought someone was following her?" Tory asked.

The manager shook his head. "No, nothing like that. I would have definitely walked her to her car if she had."

"Would she have told you?"

"Probably not. She was a good worker, and we got along well, but we didn't talk about personal matters."

"Who would she have confided in? Did she have any coworkers she considered friends?"

"Liddy and Katie were close. She's another one of the waitresses."

"Is Katie working today?"

"Sure, she's here," Dwayne said, standing. "I'll go get her."

"Poor guy," Tory murmured as he shuffled away. "He'll regret not seeing her to her car from now on."

Matt agreed. Dwayne Hobbs struck him as a decent person, and it should have been safe for a young woman to walk to her car alone after work, but he'd seen too much to believe it was, even when there wasn't a serial killer prowling around.

A twenty-something woman slid into the seat her boss had vacated. "Mr. Hobbs said that you wanted to ask me some questions. Am I in trouble?"

Tory smiled, and her features softened. "No, Katie. We're gathering information about Liddy Martin. Mr. Hobbs said you two were friends."

Katie pushed a strand of hair behind her ear and nervously licked her lips. "Why do you want to talk about Liddy? Is she in trouble?"

Matt saw Tory's shoulders tense before she broke the news. "Liddy was killed last night. We found her body on the Trace earlier today."

Katie gasped, her eyes filling with tears. "Liddy's gone? Are you sure it was her?"

"Her family identified her," Tory said gently. She laid a hand on the younger woman's arm as she wept for a few minutes.

When Katie pulled herself together, Tory asked, "When did you last see or speak with her?"

"Last night. I worked the afternoon shift, and our hours overlapped. She was fine when I left here at six."

"Her sister told us that Liddy thought someone might be following her. Did she ever mention that to you?"

Katie's eyes widened. "Yes, she did. She said she was getting the creeps. Thought some guy had followed her from her college for the past two days."

"Did Liddy mention his name, or whether she knew him?"

"She had no idea. Liddy said she didn't even really get a good look at him and, at first, she thought she was being paranoid. I guess she wasn't, was she?" Katie added sadly.

Tory handed the young woman a business card. "Call this number if you think of anything else that might be helpful." She reached out and briefly patted Katie's hand. "And please be careful out there."

Matt had asked Tory not to mention that a serial killer was on the loose. She didn't, but he could see she wanted to warn everyone she came into contact with to be vigilant.

But it wouldn't be a good idea to go public with the details yet. They had to refrain from starting a panic in town. Not only would it seriously complicate their investigation, it might drive away the killer before he'd finished his cycle, and then their investigation would be back to square one. Matt also didn't want the information released because he didn't want to give the murderer any additional press. Matt's profile indicated that the criminal craved the attention and thrived on creating chaos. He wanted recognition for his work, and Matt was going to make certain he got as little as possible.

Yet he couldn't simply ignore the threat to other women in town either.

They thanked Katie, then interviewed the other employees, but obtained no new leads about who might have been following Liddy in the days before her death.

As they walked back to the SUV, Tory brought up the issue. "News about Liddy Martin's murder is going to spread, Matt. We have to issue a statement so people know there's a predator out there."

He would have preferred to keep the investigation as quiet as possible, but it was a small town and Tory was right—news would spread about the murder. They owed a duty to the public, but he was still worried about giving the killer the attention he craved. "Let's issue a statement about the murder and warn people to be vigilant. But I want to keep as tight a lid on this as possible. I don't want any mention of a possible serial killer or the other murders, and we need to make sure no one on the task force will leak any details of this investigation."

"Okay." She placed a call to the deputy they'd left in charge at the task force office.

While she handled that, Matt took in the sights and sounds of downtown. He'd grown up there and remembered the smell of the Mississippi mingled with the music and the scent of Southern cuisine. The sound of carriages touring historic homes mixed with the more modern noise of cars on the streets. If he closed his eyes, he could hear the whistles of the steamboats floating up and down the river.

It was a nice getaway, and tourists enjoyed the history of his hometown, but Matt had never been one for dwelling on the past. He preferred to keep his eyes open and focus on the problems of the day.

They walked past a store, and he spotted a book in the window—*The True Story of the Black Creek Killer*—next to a sign noting how a local had been instrumental in capturing him. The Black Creek Killer had been Matt's first national case.

Tory stopped and glanced at it through the front window. "That was some case, Matt. I remember hearing about it. It made you famous."

"That's the case that jump-started my career."

She flashed him a genuine smile, even if it did have a hint of sadness attached to it. "I'm glad to see you're doing so well with the FBI. You wanted to be an agent for a long time."

It had always been his dream to work for the FBI, and he'd worked hard to make it happen. But it didn't escape him that it had come at a cost, and that cost was standing right in front of him.

He'd dated occasionally throughout the years, but no one had captured his heart the way Tory Mills had. They'd been best friends in school before becoming a couple, and leaving her behind had never been in his plans. He'd wanted her with him but hadn't been able to pull her away from her beloved home in Natchez. He'd assured himself that he would forget her, and although he'd managed to push her from his mind for a while, the moment he'd laid eyes on her again, he'd realized that he had never truly gotten over her.

But acting on that was a lesson in futility. He still lived and worked across the country, and she was still rooted in Natchez.

A mouthwatering scent floated their way, and his stomach growled. "Why don't we grab some lunch before continuing?" They had a lot of work to do, but he couldn't remember the last time he'd eaten, and it wasn't easy to walk past the enticing aromas coming out of the restaurants in downtown Natchez.

"Sure. Mama Shug's is right around the corner. They have home cooking if that's what you're in the mood for."

His stomach growled again. "That sounds amazing."

They walked down the street, and Tory pointed out the restaurant. He knew the place, but it had gone by a different name and likely had changed ownership in the fifteen years since he'd been away. He held the door as they stepped inside, and the hostess greeted them with a friendly smile. She seated them right away, and he ordered the special—meat loaf, mashed potatoes and gravy, and a biscuit—with an iced sweet tea. The first sip tasted like home. A guy couldn't get sweet tea like that anywhere in the country except the South.

Sitting with her sent him back to the days when reaching across the table to hold her hand was instinctive. He held back that longing, and the gulf between them seemed wider than the Mississippi River.

There had to be something they could talk about that wouldn't make him feel like a gawky kid trying to impress a girl. But not work. He didn't like talking about killers at the dinner table. "The guy who wrote that book about the Black Creek Killer? He based everything on a few local detectives who were there when the FBI was called in to the case. I wasn't even a part of it."

"Really?"

He grinned. "I had an agent contact me to tell me the author was writing the book, and asked if I wanted to be a part of it. I was busy and couldn't spare the time, so I said no. I didn't think any more about it either until the book released. It didn't occur to me at the time that anyone might want to read about catching criminals and investigative techniques." He shrugged. "I guess I was wrong. I think it recently hit the bestseller list."

She laughed at his naivety, and the sweet sound sent him reeling. It was magical, and it transported him to a time when his days consisted mostly of being with her.

"I guess you were wrong," Tory said. "Lots of people are interested in true crime these days. Even me."

"I've actually had several publishers reach out to ask if I'd want to write about how I solved some of my cases. I have to admit, it's an idea that's piqued my interest. I'm considering doing it." He couldn't explain why he felt the need to spill that information, but he wanted her to know. He'd worked hard to become the best in his field, and it felt good to have the recognition in Tory's eyes.

She took a sip of her tea. "That's a book I'd read."

"Would you really?"

"You bet. Janet, at the bookstore, tells me whenever a new book about one of your cases comes out." Her face reddened as she realized she'd admitted to keeping up with his career.

It surprised him, since it was his career that had torn them apart. He wasn't embarrassed by it, but she must have been, as she stumbled to recover.

"I, um, like to read about true crime cases in general. Not only yours. I enjoy reading about how cases get solved, and I really enjoy studying the process of profiling. I think we can all learn a thing or two about that in our work. True crime is kind of a hobby of mine."

Matt drank some more tea to hide his smile. It felt good to hear that she'd thought about him over the years, no matter how she tried to dismiss it.

He'd mulled over the book idea for ages, but he finally came to a decision.

At least, he knew of one person who would read it.

$\mathcal{T}$ory took a big gulp of her iced tea and did her best to hide the flush creeping into her cheeks. She couldn't believe she'd given away the fact that she'd kept up with Matt's career. The words had slipped out. She'd meant to say that she liked all kinds of true crime books, not just books about him.

And Matt wore a smug smile over her obvious embarrassment. Humiliation morphed into irritation.

Why was she worried about what Matt Shepherd thought about her?

She decided to refocus attention on him instead. "How does it feel being back in Natchez after all this time?"

He took a bite of his mashed potatoes. "The food is still great, obviously. Downtown hasn't changed much in over a hundred years, so I guess it wouldn't in fifteen, would it?"

She loved that the town didn't change. Tourists came year after year to be transported back in time, and Tory loved that Natchez continued to provide such an experience. They had updated in some ways, of course. Crime had increased. And the casino brought a new stream of revenue, yet they still managed to maintain that historic, small-town flavor.

Her first job out of high school had been working as an interpretive ranger for the National Park Service. She'd provided tours of the Natchez Trace historical sites and had enjoyed that job. It was when the opportunity to become a law enforcement ranger presented itself that she had reevaluated her goals and chosen to go through the training.

She still got to be a part of the Trace, but she also helped safeguard it.

"Do you ever miss it here?" She held her breath and watched his reaction to her question. It sounded much more personal than she'd intended, as if she were asking if he missed *her*. They'd had good times there together.

"I do miss it sometimes," he admitted. "Especially after a big case. I've seen a lot of bad things in my job. Then I think about Natchez and how simple life was here for me. All places have their share of crime and troubles, but Natchez has always felt like home."

She was glad to hear him say that. Her worst fear had been that he'd left home and never looked back, never thought of her at all. Irrational, yes, but the idea had bothered her especially when she'd seen how successful he was with the FBI.

"It certainly does for me," she agreed. "I love the idea of walking the same streets as my ancestors. You're right that crime has increased, and the casino moved in, but every day I can still smell the river and hear the clip-clop of the horse hooves taking tourists around, and I think about how those are the same sounds and smells my grandparents and my great-grandparents enjoyed. It makes me feel connected to them and to this town." Her family had been in Natchez for six generations, and there was no other place she'd ever wanted to live. Even when her father died and her mom had gone to live with her sister—Tory's aunt—in Shreveport, Louisiana, Tory hadn't considered moving.

Natchez was her home, and she couldn't imagine that ever changing.

Matt straightened in his chair. "I'm plenty aware of how much you love this town. It's the reason you didn't want to come with me all those years ago. It's the reason you broke off our engagement. I never could compete with Natchez." A hint of pain shone on his face.

"It wasn't a competition, Matt. This is my home. I loved it here, and I loved my job as much as you loved being in the FBI." But that wasn't the entire reason she'd said no to moving away with him, and she owed him the truth. "Besides, I knew how ambitious you were back then, and I never doubted that you would succeed. I also understood that, when that happened, I would be left behind while you traveled for work. I didn't want to be abandoned in Virginia or Washington or some other place where I had no one to depend on, while you were away on your latest case. And I was right too, wasn't I? How often are you actually at your home?"

His jaw clenched, and his cheeks reddened a bit. "Not a lot, to be honest. My cleaning service sees my apartment more often than I do." He gave a weary sigh. "If I can be frank, it's beginning to take a toll. Not only the traveling—it's everything. In my job, I see the worst of human beings. It takes me to a dark place mentally, and it keeps me there for far too long. It gets a little harder to haul myself out of it after each case, and I'm afraid that one day I won't be able to get back out at all."

The toll was evident on his face, and her heart went out to him. She nearly reached across the table to take his hand to comfort him, when someone approached their table. She pulled her hand away. No need for the gossip rumor mill to spread. And, besides, he'd chosen his work over her. It was too late to change that.

"Why, Tory Mills. It's good to see you."

She glanced up as Chelsea Morrison, an acquaintance from her church, approached the table. Tory instantly went on alert. Chelsea worked for *Natchez News*, a local paper, and Matt had warned her to be careful not to spill information about a possible serial killer in town.

"Hello, Chelsea. It's good to see you too."

"Who's your friend?" Chelsea smiled at Matt and held out her hand. "Chelsea Morrison, reporter for *Natchez News*."

"Nice to meet you," Matt responded. "Matt Shepherd."

Her features feigned surprise, and Tory guessed she'd known exactly who she was talking to before she'd even walked over. She and Chelsea hardly had the type of relationship where they spoke each time they met around town. "Not *the* Matthew Shepherd? The FBI agent who captured the Black River Killer? Why, I purchased a book about you the other day. I heard the FBI was in town, and I'd love to interview you about this newest investigation. I presume there is an investigation that's brought you here."

Tory cringed at the woman's brazenness, but Matt didn't miss a beat.

"I'm sorry, but I really don't have the time. Plus, I can't comment on open investigations." His practiced tone was all business, and Tory suspected he was used to dealing with the press.

"Surely you can spare some time to talk about your other investigations, for your hometown paper."

"I really can't."

"Oh, come on," Chelsea pressed.

"He said no, Chelsea," Tory interjected. She didn't like being rude, but Chelsea could be impossibly dogged, whether she was trying to get a photograph of someone's prized roses for the garden section of the paper, or trying to coerce an interview out of an FBI agent who happened to arrive in town.

Chelsea scowled at Tory, then forced her smile back into place. "No problem. Nice to meet you, Agent Shepherd. Tory, I'll speak to you at church." She sauntered away.

Tory wasn't looking forward to the conversation, certain she was in for an earful, but she couldn't bow to the whim of other people, especially on such an important matter as a murder investigation. If Matt changed his mind and decided to give Chelsea an interview, Tory wouldn't get in the middle of it. But if Chelsea was already snooping around, did that mean their business had already been leaked somehow?

Matt leaned forward, lowering his voice. "I'm sorry if I was rude to your friend. I don't want to give this perp any more notoriety than I'm forced to."

Tory understood his logic. There was only one problem—Natchez was still very much a small town. "Keeping it a secret will be harder to do if another body is discovered."

"That's another reason we have to find the killer before that happens," Matt said. "I want to go check out the campgrounds. Our perpetrator moves from national park to national park. It's possible he's transitory, living out of an RV or camping off the land."

Tory's cell phone buzzed with a message from her neighbor. It was unusual for him to text her so she read the message. One of her dogs was limping and appeared to have been injured, but wouldn't let the neighbor get near enough to examine him.

"Is something wrong?" Matt asked.

"It's my neighbor. One of my dogs might be hurt, so I need to go home."

"I'll drive you back to your vehicle, then wait for you at the sheriff's office while you make sure he's okay."

She agreed and he paid the bill, then they hurried from the restaurant and climbed into Matt's SUV for the ride back to her vehicle. She hated to leave Matt in the middle of an investigation, but her neighbor wasn't one to jump to conclusions. If he thought something was amiss with her dog, he was probably right.

Matt parked at the sheriff's office and cut the engine. "I'll meet you back here, and then we'll get started. Hopefully, your dog is okay."

"Thank you. I'll get back as soon as I can." She hopped out, rushed to her own cruiser, and headed toward her house.

Home was a small two-bedroom cabin off the highway, north of the city limits. Sitting on half an acre of land and backed by woods, it provided a feeling of rural living with modern amenities available in a short drive. Her nearest neighbor lived within shouting distance, though she rarely actually saw him, and the wooded area behind her house provided plenty of land for hiking, camping, and hunting.

She pulled off the road and into her driveway. Her three dogs greeted the vehicle, barking and jumping and darting around. She loved coming home to the excitement of her three rescue pups and was thankful she lived in a location where the dogs could spend time outdoors without being in danger of getting into heavy traffic. Tory had a covered porch with plenty of shade and a fan to keep them cool when they were outside, and her neighbor kept an eye on them whenever she had to work crazy hours, so she never had to worry about her furry friends being fed or cared for.

Bet I couldn't find that living in a big city full of strangers rather than family and friends.

It was one of many reasons she loved Natchez.

She knelt down to pet each dog. Jojo, her fifty-pound Labrador retriever mix, and Bingo, her midsize blue heeler mix, were obviously fine. Her third dog, Bob, was an unusual concoction of German shepherd and Chihuahua. She often said he resembled something someone had cooked up in a lab. He was bigger than a Chihuahua, but still small enough to leap into her arms and be carried around. She noticed he was limping, and she examined him, spotting a cut on one of his back legs. He'd probably gotten into something in the woods behind her house.

After she'd greeted the dogs, Jojo and Bingo began panting heavily and running and barking at the tree line near the woods. Even Bob leaped from her arms and took off to follow his sisters, his speed barely hindered, indicating that the injury couldn't be too painful. They were particularly riled up at something. Probably an animal lurking in the brush—maybe even the critter Bob had tangled with. She followed them around the cabin but saw nothing that would upset them. Bingo, who was usually the first one to dart into the woods after a squirrel, stood back from the edge of the trees, barking and showing her teeth. The other two remained behind her, also barking but unwilling to go any deeper into the trees.

The hairs on the back of Tory's neck rose, and a shudder ran through her. She spun around, her eyes darting back and forth, her instincts on high alert. She saw nothing but was certain she felt someone watching her. She couldn't ignore her gut, and she couldn't discount her pups' reactions either.

She drew her gun from its holster and walked the perimeter of the house, searching for anything or anyone that might be causing such unrest. She saw no movement in the brush, nothing that appeared to be a threat.

She wound up back at the front porch where she'd started. Nothing was outside. Had she imagined that feeling of being watched? The dogs didn't seem to think so. They continued to pant and growl, sticking close to her.

Tory held her breath as she stepped onto the porch and opened the door, alert in case someone was lurking inside. She moved through the cabin and cleared each room.

Nothing.

She holstered her gun and brought the dogs inside. They soon settled down, shifting their focus from guarding the house to holding down the couch while she cleaned and bandaged Bob's leg. She didn't know what had gotten them so worked up, but it was likely nothing more than a raccoon in the woods.

And her own discomfort?

Well, there was a serial killer in town, and that knowledge was a lot to deal with. It probably had her jumpier than usual.

Also, there was seeing Matt again after all those years. He was every bit as attractive as ever, if not more so. Seeing him had shaken her. She couldn't deny it, but neither could she allow a random feeling of what might have been to affect her job.

They'd had a nice lunch, and that had stirred up some old emotions for her, but they had a murderer to catch, so personal feelings would have to be set aside. A killer was on the loose in her hometown, and it was up to her and Matt to find him before he murdered again.

She stared at herself in her bathroom mirror and blew out a breath, wondering why seeing Matt Shepherd again had shaken her more than learning a serial killer was lurking around the corner.

6

*W*hile he waited for Tory to meet him at the sheriff's office, Matt typed up his notes, going back over the details of the scene where Liddy Martin had been found, comparing it with the other scenes. As he'd thought, the similarities were undeniable. He didn't see anything to make him believe it wasn't the work of the same killer.

Matt noted the time on his phone and also found a new text message from Tory that everything was fine. She should be back soon so they could start investigating the RV parks. He opened his laptop and printed off a list of names and vehicle registration numbers he'd previously compiled from the other crime scenes.

He glanced up and saw two deputies surreptitiously watching him as they chatted over a cup of coffee. He acknowledged them before turning back to his work. It wasn't unusual to have local officers curious about his methods. Most of the law enforcement he'd encountered over the course of his career had been easy to work with, and the local police in Natchez were no different.

He spotted Tory's SUV through the window as she slid into a parking space. Hurrying out to meet her, he found that he was getting used to seeing her with her hair back, and he was beginning to like it. When he yanked his mind back to the matter at hand, he could see that she was pale and seemed shaken, which put him on instant alert. "Everything okay?"

Had something happened when she went home to see to her pets?

"It's fine." But her voice betrayed a hint of worry.

"Tory, what's going on?"

"It's nothing." Even her insistence sounded hollow. He recognized her expression. She was trying to play it cool, but something had rattled her. Maybe no one else would notice it, but he did. After all, he'd once known her face better than any other.

He touched her arm. "Tory, it's me. Tell me what happened."

She jutted out her chin in defiance, but she belied the gesture by biting her lip. Finally, she lowered her head. "It's probably nothing, but my dogs were all upset when I arrived home, as if someone had been at my house."

He stiffened at the idea that she might have walked in on an intruder. "Did you call the police? Do we need to go there?"

"I inspected the house inside and out. No one was there. The dogs were probably barking at a raccoon or something in the woods. I called and asked my neighbor to keep an eye out though. We've had some burglaries in town." She took a deep breath to calm herself. "I'm fine. Really, I am. Now, where are we?"

He wasn't ready to move on from her scare, but she obviously was. He didn't like the idea that someone might have broken into her home but reminded himself that Tory Mills was a trained law enforcement officer who could take care of herself. In fact, he pitied anyone who broke in while she was there. That wouldn't end well for the intruder.

He took out his list and handed it to her. "I compiled this list of driver's licenses and vehicle registrations from people who were present at each of the national parks around the time of the murders. It's about ten people. So far, I haven't been able to find any connections, so there's no guarantee the killer is even on this list. Our killer is definitely in the area, so I want to visit the RV parks in the vicinity and see if we can track down any from the list here in Natchez."

"What makes you think he's traveling in an RV?"

"He's moving around the country from park to park. It makes sense to me that he might be traveling in one. And I added the driver's licenses to the list, just in case."

She scanned the record. "Well, there are several campgrounds in and around Natchez that accept RV parking. The Bluff City RV Park is close to town for an easy walk to shops and dining."

"We can go, but it's doubtful he'd stay so near. He would probably want more privacy."

"Then there's Natchez Camping farther out, and Pebble Springs Campground on the Trace." She frowned. "Actually, Pebble Springs is a free campground. There are no fees. No license requirements, no reservations required. Nothing to compare to your list."

Most campgrounds required some kind of identification and fee in order to enter and park or camp, so her revelation disappointed him. "Don't the rangers keep tabs on these things?"

"Periodically, but we don't document every vehicle. In fact, there's a ranger station right at the entrance to the campground, but it's been closed for years. No one mans it any longer. We patrol the area as best we can, but we've got a limited number of rangers and forty miles of road to manage."

Which, in his mind, seemed an ideal area for their suspect to go unnoticed. "We'll still look," he told her.

Tory slid behind the wheel of her cruiser, and Matt took the passenger seat. They decided to check out the Bluff City RV Park first because it was the closest. She stopped at the front office, and they spoke with the manager on duty, who gave them a sign-in log of names and tag numbers for everyone currently parked there. Matt compared the document to his list but found no matching registrations. He thanked the manager, then handed back her sign-in sheet. Their killer wasn't there. Tory and Matt drove through the park to be sure but saw nothing which raised their suspicions.

They had the same luck at Natchez Camping. The manager provided a list of people who'd signed in and paid the RV fees. None matched Matt's data.

Tory headed north to Pebble Springs Campground. Matt spotted a sign for the site, which was near the turnoff, and noted the abandoned ranger post she'd mentioned.

Another sign directed them to keep straight to access the trails and the old, abandoned town of Pebble Springs, or take a right toward the camping area. Memories flooded back to Matt. He and Tory had hiked the trails there many times, including the original, lowered path people had traveled on their way back to the north hundreds of years ago, after sailing their goods down the Mississippi to the Natchez port. What was left of the town had been mostly ruins even fifteen years before, except for a wooden church that still stood and, to his knowledge, still provided Sunday morning services, but it was the markers and the history behind the place that drew tourists.

Tory steered toward the campground. Many of the spots were occupied by RVs as they drove the circular road through the site. They parked near a group of RVs clustered close together and several people gathered around a firepit, though the sky wasn't yet completely dark.

"Maybe they can give us some information," Tory said as they got out.

The entire group studied Matt and Tory, two of them standing as they drew nearer. There were at least two other couples, along with a handful of kids.

Matt showed his credentials.

"FBI?" asked one of the adults. "Is there a problem, Ranger?"

"No problem," Matt said. "We're simply making sure things are going all right. How long have you all been here?"

"We arrived yesterday afternoon," one man explained. "We're here for an archery tournament and decided to take some tours."

"Do you recognize any of these names?" Matt took the list of names and registration numbers from his jacket and handed it to the man.

He scanned them as the woman beside him read over his shoulder. "I don't recognize anyone," he stated. He glanced at the woman for confirmation and she shook her head.

"What about anyone suspicious? Have any of you noticed anything strange?"

Another woman sitting near the firepit stood. "Yes, last night." She handed the child in her arms to a third woman before walking over. "We saw a white truck. The driver parked up on the hill and apparently slept in his truck. My husband approached him to see if we could help him with anything. We had some extra food from grilling last night, and we thought he might be homeless and living in his vehicle, but he told my husband he was fine. The truck was gone this morning when we woke up."

That piqued Matt's interest. A man in a white truck, as witnesses had reported fleeing the scene where Liddy Martin had been found? If it was the same pickup, they'd finally caught a break in the case. "Can you describe the man or give any further details about the truck?"

"I couldn't tell his height because he was sitting, but he was of average build. Around forty. Dark hair. I took a photo of the license plate."

"You did?" Matt did his best to contain the excitement in his voice. He was thankful for vigilant witnesses.

"I told you, something about him was off. I try to be helpful if I can, but I'm not going to risk anything happening around my kids." She retrieved her cell phone and showed the photo to Matt, who copied down the numbers.

"Thank you," he told the woman. "This is a big help."

Matt and Tory hurried back to Tory's SUV, and she started off down the Trace.

"The man this group saw matches the description given of the suspect seen running from the scene where Liddy's body was found." Matt took out his cell phone but had little service. He tried dialing the sheriff's office anyway, anxious to get someone on the task force to research identification for the tag number. However, the call wouldn't go through.

"Give it time," she said when he growled in frustration. "We'll find a signal the closer we get to a town that intersects with the parkway."

Matt couldn't help his impatience. They had a good lead and a simple lack of cell phone service was stopping him from moving forward. The thirty-minute drive back to Natchez seemed to stretch for hours.

Finally, his call went through.

He spoke with one of the deputies Sheriff Ford had assigned to his task force. "Can you get me an identification on a car tag? Louisiana plates." He read out the number, then waited as the deputy typed it into a computer.

"The registration is in the name of a Victor Lance. He has a Louisiana address right across the river. Says here he's a long-haul trucker by occupation."

If he wasn't on the job, he would be using his personal vehicle instead of his big rig to drive into Natchez. "I'll need that address, along with a team to visit his house."

The deputy promised to assemble a team before Matt ended the call. "This may be our break," he told Tory.

"You really think this guy could have been living here all along?"

"He's a long-haul trucker, which means he could have traveled all over the country, maybe even close to the other national parks. And he's suddenly back in town at the same time the killer is here? I don't believe in coincidences like that."

"So maybe our killer is a big rig truck driver instead of an RVer like you thought."

"Could be." It made as much sense as anything else. He was grateful to have something concrete to investigate at last.

The team was already loading up two SUVs when Matt and Tory arrived back at the sheriff's office. Matt grabbed his vest from the back of his SUV, then gave orders to the team. "We're going to find this guy and bring him in. He could be a suspect in multiple murders. For now, all we have are witnesses who saw him fleeing Liddy Martin's crime scene. Don't jump to conclusions, but be prepared. He should be considered dangerous as a precaution."

Matt climbed back into Tory's SUV and rode with her while the rest of the team filled two other vehicles. He could feel the anticipation pouring off her as she drove across the bridge linking Mississippi and Louisiana. He was anxious too, but it was a productive kind of edginess, eager to move forward on the case and get closer to capturing a killer.

During the drive, Matt alerted local Louisiana law enforcement that they were coming, and a cruiser met him and Tory at the end of the road for the address they'd been given.

Tory pulled up beside the patrol car and rolled down the window. "Have you seen our suspect?"

"No. I drove past the address and saw no one outside. However, there are two vehicles in the driveway and lights on in the house."

She thanked him and continued down the street to the address the GPS had identified. They wound up in the driveway of a house with a dilapidated front porch, on a patch of land in the middle of what felt like nowhere.

Matt scanned the woods surrounding the lot—no neighbors within shouting distance. Their perpetrator could abduct and murder someone out there with no one the wiser. There were plenty of places to hide bodies in the woods too, which made the killer's desire to dump them in park grounds all the more perplexing. Unless he was, as Matt suspected, intentionally trying to have them found.

Tory and Matt got out of the vehicle as the rest of the team parked behind them and did the same. Matt approached the house, but his guard was on high alert. It didn't escape his attention that there was no semitruck parked anywhere in sight, but it could have been hidden behind the house. He also didn't see the white pickup truck that had led them there. Only an old sedan and an SUV with stickers on the back window indicating that there were kids on board.

The possibility of children being present made Matt uncomfortable. He radioed his team to be watchful. He didn't want anyone misfiring and hitting a little one as they searched for Victor Lance.

"It looks perfectly normal," Tory commented. She drew her weapon and kept it lowered as they approached the house.

"Looks can be deceiving."

Matt knew that better than anyone. The Black River Killer had been a family man, whose wife and teenage kids had been stunned when Matt arrested him. The killer's family had claimed to have no idea about his sinister activity, even though he'd kept trophies in their basement.

Matt stepped onto the old porch, knocking on the door as Tory stood at the bottom of the steps.

He heard the sound of children inside and a woman hollering at them to be quiet. Finally, she opened the door. She appeared thin and tired, and Matt spotted at least three kids under eight, running circles in the visible living room area.

"Can I help you?"

He showed her his badge. "I'm Special Agent Matt Shepherd with the FBI. This is Ranger Tory Mills. We have to talk to Victor Lance. Is he home?"

Her eyes narrowed in obvious suspicion, and she placed a hand on her hip. "Why? What did he do?"

Matt didn't flinch. "We have to speak with him, ma'am."

She stepped onto the porch and closed the door behind her. That's when she spotted the other vehicles and officers with guns surrounding her house. "What's happening? What did he do?"

"Can you tell us where Victor Lance is? Is he your spouse?"

"He is, but I kicked him out over a week ago. I haven't seen him since."

"Any ideas where he might have gone?" Matt asked.

She snorted. "Probably to the casino. That's where he spent most of his time anyway, when he wasn't on the road."

"I don't see a semi here. Is it possible he's on a job?"

"The trucking company repossessed it a month ago. Apparently, when he was supposed to be working, he was out gambling instead. Check across the river in Natchez. That's where I'd start."

"You understand we can't just take your word for it," Tory told her.

Mrs. Lance stepped back and waved them in. "Help yourself. He's not here."

The team did their best to cover the house quickly, ultimately finding nothing but a family dealing with the fallout of an absent husband and father.

"Are you done?" Mrs. Lance demanded as they finished up. "I need to feed, bathe, and put my kids to bed. They have school tomorrow."

Matt handed her his business card with his cell phone on it. "Call me if you hear from your husband. It's important."

She glanced at his card. "What's this about, Agent Shepherd?"

He felt a duty to warn Victor Lance's wife that her husband could be dangerous. She'd kicked the man out, and it was important that she not allow him back around her or the kids. "It could be about murder, Mrs. Lance."

Her eyes widened, and her mouth sprang open in surprise. "I mean, Victor's a bad husband, and he's not such a great father either, but he's not a killer."

"Call me if you hear from him," Matt repeated.

"Okay." Mrs. Lance closed the door, and he heard the lock click into place.

She hadn't believed him. Thankfully, he didn't have to sit around and wait for her call. "Let's get tracking on Lance's cell phone. If his wife calls him, I want to know about it. We can also use GPS or cell phone tower data to try to pinpoint his location with it."

"Lance doesn't have his big rig anymore," Tory pointed out as they returned to her vehicle. "If those people at the campground are right, he's living in his pickup, so he's unlikely to remain in one place."

"Actually, that might work in our favor. Pebble Springs is free and out of the way. Sounds to me like the perfect place for Lance to return to," Matt responded.

"Except for that vigilant witness—the mom—who was watching his every move to keep her kids safe."

"There are a lot of places in that campground where he could park out of their view," Matt countered. "Besides, if the mom does see him, I expect she'll call me." Victor Lance was shaping up to be a reasonable suspect. "Let's add Lance's name and license number to the BOLO. Can we have a ranger patrol that area more closely tonight?"

"I'm sure Chris can arrange it," Tory said.

"Good. I also want to try the casino. If his wife is right, Lance might be there."

"Unless he's run out of money," Tory said. "He's unemployed and homeless now."

"Then let's pray he's on a winning streak."

Matt made the necessary calls as Tory drove back across the river and to the casino parking lot. It was full, and they located three white pickups, but none matched the description and license plate number they had.

Tory sighed, giving voice to the same frustration Matt was feeling. "What do you want to do now?"

"He's probably not here, but let's go inside anyway. He might have sold or ditched the truck."

She parked and they entered the casino. Matt wandered the floor, bar, and gaming areas while Tory met up with security personnel. He didn't find anyone who resembled the driver's license photo they had of Lance. He finally admitted defeat and reconnected with Tory.

"I don't see him," Matt said.

Tory's eyebrows rose. "Well, security recognized him. He's been playing the blackjack tables and losing a lot recently. I gave them my number. If Lance comes back, they'll notify us."

It was the best they were going to get for the night, unless something hit on the BOLO. He massaged his temples, idly wondering whether true crime books would sell as well if they documented all the tedium, the false leads, the dead ends in every investigation.

"Let's head back to the sheriff's office. I want to pull Victor Lance's financials. I also want to contact his trucking company and get his driving logs. If he's been near any of the other national park crime scenes, they'll tell us."

Tory glanced at her watch. "I doubt you'll be able to get in touch with them tonight. It's already after ten p.m."

"First thing tomorrow, then." Matt hated to wait, but she was right. Besides, he would need a warrant for the trucking company's records anyway, and no judge was going to sign off on that so close to midnight.

He was disappointed that they hadn't found Lance yet, but at least they had a name—finally, a lead that might actually go somewhere.

*T*ory paced back and forth in the conference room at the sheriff's office. Sleep had eluded her all night as she ruminated over how close they'd come to capturing Victor Lance the day before.

There were no hits on the BOLO overnight, and Lance's financial records hadn't revealed anything suspicious. The man had very little money in his accounts, so Tory and Matt were left to assume he was using cash to get by. Tory contacted the trucking company first thing that morning, but as Matt had suspected, they required time—and a warrant—in order to put together the requested files, which frustrated her. Many modern trucking companies used electronic logs, but of course the one Lance worked for was behind the times.

Matt was busy typing up his notes from their interviews. She could tell from the dark circles under his eyes that he hadn't gotten much sleep either. He'd checked into a hotel to shower and change clothes, but she suspected that he, too, had been up most of the night. In fact, he'd beaten her into the sheriff's office that morning.

Tory probably should have been documenting her notes rather than pacing, but she hoped to come up with something that would move the investigation along before another woman was murdered.

Learning that the offender killed in threes and was likely already stalking his next victim had rattled her. She was anxious to do something, but what?

She stalked over to where Matt was working. "I don't understand how you can be so calm. I'm about ready to jump out of my skin with all this waiting."

He rubbed his chin. "Unfortunately, waiting is part of the game. We can't always get what we want when we want it. Not even with the FBI to open doors for us. In the meantime, we've got patrols out looking for Victor Lance, and a BOLO on his pickup. He'll have to pop his head out eventually."

"You really think this guy is our killer?"

Matt closed his laptop and leaned back in his chair. "It's a good lead. Witnesses saw him and his truck fleeing from the crime scene, and he matches the description they gave. It does bother me that he's local, though. I was really thinking this killer was either an RVer or lived off the land, but I suppose his being a long-haul trucker makes sense too. However, it would be pretty coincidental if the killer and I were both from the same area."

She hadn't considered that. Natchez was Matt's hometown, and Victor Lance was from a town right across the river. Perhaps that was the reason the killer felt a connection with the FBI agent chasing him. Another thought hit her. "That would make a great twist in your book though."

"It sure would."

An idea suddenly sprang to mind. "What if this guy could live off the land?"

"It's possible," Matt answered, his tone musing. "If he takes his victims into the woods to kill them before dumping their bodies in areas where they would be found, as the evidence seems to show, he would need privacy for that and at least a few survival skills. Besides, some of the places where we found bodies were not easily accessible, suggesting an experienced wilderness traveler."

"Well, if he's camping on the Trace, then he's breaking the law. We aren't like other national parks. Camping here must be done in specific, designated areas."

"So we put out a notice to the rangers to be on the lookout for someone camping illegally? It couldn't hurt."

"I was also thinking we could use heat-sensing cameras to scan the Trace. It would only take a few hours to scan fifty miles or so if we use a helicopter."

Excitement built in his features. "That's a great idea. Do the rangers have access to a helicopter?"

"We can borrow one from the Forestry Service or the Department of Public Safety. It might take some time to procure, but we should be able to get out there by this afternoon." She figured it had to be more productive than sitting around waiting for something to happen.

A grin spread over his face. "Excellent idea, Tory. You set that up. I'll see about finding a heat-sensing camera."

By lunchtime, they had a chopper ready to go. Matt climbed aboard the helicopter, then reached back to help her in. She was still basking a little in the glow of his approval of her plan and really hoped her idea yielded something they could use.

Tory had been trained to use the cameras to search for poachers. It wasn't particularly unusual to find someone illegally hunting deer on protected land, and one of her jobs was to monitor such things.

"We're ready," Matt instructed the pilot. He'd previously briefed the pilot on what they were doing and where to fly, so Tory activated the camera and used it to hunt for heat signals.

After flying over fifty miles of parkland, they'd seen plenty of wildlife and trees but hadn't found a single human heat source coming from the protected woods.

Tory was disappointed at their results, and she could see Matt was too.

"I'm sorry," she said, as the pilot landed the helicopter and they stepped off. "I thought that might reveal something."

He patted her shoulder. "It was a good idea that didn't pan out. We're no worse off now than we were earlier in the day. In fact, we're better because we've crossed that off our list of places the killer might be camping. We can move on from here."

She was thankful for his understanding, but she couldn't help feeling as if they'd wasted precious time.

Tory and Matt drove back to the sheriff's office and checked in with the rest of the team. So far, there had been no hits on the BOLO or on the alerts she'd placed on Victor Lance's financials. If he was spending money, he was using cash.

"Has the tech team been able to track Lance's cell phone yet?" she asked a deputy.

"There's been no activity so far. Wherever he is, he must have it off or taken out the battery. This guy is doing his best to lay low."

More disappointing news.

She ventured a glance at Matt, who was talking on his cell phone. She sensed his frustration that the case wasn't moving despite the line he'd given her about patience. Patience was not a trait either one of them possessed, and that could always be a downfall in their line of work. But how could they be patient? Another woman's life was at risk. In fact, based on the murderer's pattern, at least two more local women if they didn't catch him soon enough. And who knew how many more if he finished his gruesome work in Natchez and moved on to terrorize another area?

A deputy approached Matt as he ended his phone call and gave him a large manila envelope. "Agent Shepherd, this was delivered for you."

Matt thanked the deputy and tore open the envelope.

Matt's jaw clenched as he removed the contents, and his entire demeanor shifted. His shoulders slumped and he groaned.

Tory hurried over to him. "What is it?"

He handed her a photograph.

Her pulse quickened at the image. It was a snapshot of her and Matt, taken as they'd stood outside the Natchez Diner the day before, after interviewing Liddy Martin's coworkers.

Four words were scrawled across the image in red lettering.

Welcome home, Agent Shepherd.

ory snatched the envelope from Matt's hand. He watched her eyes widen as she stared at the image—proof that they were being followed and watched by the killer.

Dread boiled in the pit of Matt's stomach. He'd placed Tory in a murderer's crosshairs.

"What is this and where did it come from?" Her tone was laced with both fury and fear. She flipped the envelope over to study the front. "There's no postmark, which means it was hand delivered. He knows we're working here." She spun around and called for the deputy who'd given Matt the envelope. "This obviously didn't come through the mail. Who delivered it?"

"Some kid dropped it off a few minutes ago. Said to give it to Agent Shepherd."

"What kid? Can you describe him?" Matt asked.

The deputy pointed through a window in the double-doored entrance to the sheriff's office. "That's him getting on a bike."

Sure enough, a teenager on the sidewalk was climbing onto a bicycle.

Tory burst through the doors and called after him. "Hey, wait up." She stopped the guy before Matt even made it to the door to follow her.

Marching the teen back into the station, Tory directed him to have a seat. He was a kid, probably no more than sixteen or seventeen if Matt had to guess. Certainly not old enough to be their killer.

Tory stood over the teen, her eyes blazing. "Who gave you this?" she demanded, and the kid flinched under her glare.

"Some guy paid me a hundred bucks. Said all I had to do was deliver that envelope to Matt Shepherd at the sheriff's office."

He shouldn't be surprised that the killer had gotten someone else to do his dirty work for him. He wouldn't get close enough for the cameras to capture him or to get himself linked to the photograph.

"What did this man look like?" Matt asked.

The teen shrugged. "He was an older guy. He approached me at the gas station on the corner. He wore sunglasses and a hat, so I couldn't really see his face. Besides, I was more focused on the money he was flashing at me."

"I assume this office has surveillance cameras," Matt said to Tory.

"Absolutely."

"Let's get our hands on the footage. Maybe we can capture an image. And have someone go up and down the street. I want any surveillance video that might have caught him. Make sure we get the footage from the gas station."

"You got it." She pointed to the kid. "You stay put. You'll have to make an identification." She took several deputies aside and gave them instructions about the surveillance videos. Facing the teen again, she added, "Oh, and we're going to need that hundred dollars he gave you."

The kid blanched. "Aw, come on. Really?"

"We might be able to get fingerprints from it."

The teen issued a frustrated sigh, then took it from his pocket and handed it to her. She placed it into an evidence bag and passed it off to another officer to hurry to the lab.

"What's your name, son?" Tory asked.

"Simon Stephens."

"Well, Simon, I'll see if the sheriff has some cash on hand. If so, I'll exchange your hundred for another."

Matt was amazed by the way Tory could be stern one moment, then soft and friendly the next. If it were him, he'd be informing the teen that he was lucky they weren't pressing charges against him for delivering a threatening note to law enforcement personnel—which would merely alienate Simon. He was suddenly very glad Tory was on his side. She'd taken control of the situation and delegated the assignments, even when he could see she was still uneasy over the photograph. As they waited for the video surveillance tapes, she picked it up again, studied it, then raised her gaze to his.

He could tell she had questions, and he wouldn't hold back if she asked. She deserved the answers, and he was still kicking himself for placing her in a murderer's path. Seeing her in that photo had unnerved him too.

But before she had a chance to ask him anything, the officers she'd sent out returned.

The deputies explained that they'd requested the surveillance videos be sent electronically, so she pulled up her email account and accessed the footage from the gas station at the corner. Everyone huddled around the screen.

Matt spotted Simon in the video, pedaling up to the store on his bike.

He stood behind Tory, watching over her shoulder, the smell of her shampoo sending his thoughts tumbling over each other. He had to keep it together and not allow himself to get distracted by her.

"That's him," Simon stated, pointing to a man on the screen. "He's the one who gave me the money and the envelope."

They watched as a man in a baseball cap and sunglasses spoke with Simon before handing him the items. Matt noticed that when the kid rode off, the man followed. He wanted to make sure his package was delivered.

"Try the surveillance from the street," Matt instructed. "He's following the kid."

"H-he followed me?" Simon stuttered. He wrung his hands. "I didn't notice."

Tory opened a different video from another angle. "He wanted to make sure you did what he asked."

She rewound the video until they spotted her parking the National Park Service SUV, and she and Matt got out and walked into the sheriff's station. Matt didn't see Simon, but he did spot the familiar clothes, hat, and sunglasses in a corner of the shot.

"There he is." He pointed to the figure. The man watched them walk inside, then turned and headed down the street in the direction of the gas station. "We'd just returned from the helipad. That's how he figured out we were here." No wonder they hadn't spotted him in the woods. He'd been watching and waiting for them.

The serial killer not only knew Matt was in town—he knew which office they were working out of.

"He planned it for right when we arrived back at the sheriff's office," Tory said. She locked eyes with him. "He was following us, Matt. He probably still is. He's monitoring our investigation."

Simon rode into the video and parked his bike, and Matt spotted the likely killer again lurking in the distance, watching until after Tory had dragged Simon back into the station. Then he walked away.

The murderer had been right under their noses and they hadn't had a clue.

"Can I go home now?" Simon asked.

Tory glanced at Matt, who dipped his chin slightly. Simon didn't have anything more to offer.

"You can go," Tory told the kid.

"What about my money?"

"Come back tomorrow. I should know by then whether or not I can replace it."

"No, wait." Matt pulled out his wallet and handed Simon a hundred-dollar bill to replace the one they'd confiscated. "Thanks for your help."

Once Simon was gone, Tory picked up the photo. "What is this, Matt?"

He took it from her and motioned for her to join him in the conference room.

When the door closed, Tory confronted him. "You told me this killer stalks his victims. Why is he stalking *us?*" She held up the photograph. "He was watching us. He sent this to you. Why?"

Matt lowered himself into a chair and did his best to choose his words wisely. "I told you before that he's reached out to me with letters. It's a good sign, Tory. Once these guys start contacting law enforcement, they're usually one step closer to being captured."

"He was one step closer to us, Matt. He could have shot us both and been done with it."

"He's taunting me, Tory, not you. The reason you even made his radar is because you were standing beside me."

She fell into a chair, and he was again stricken with guilt that he'd dragged her into such a mess. The killer hadn't been aware of Tory before Matt returned to town. It wasn't the first time someone had gotten caught up in the game this offender wanted to play with Matt, but it was the first time someone he personally cared for was involved.

Matt leaned forward. "I'm so sorry, Tory. This has been going on for a while now. I was hoping his communication with me would help me get closer to him. Instead, *he's* getting closer to *me.*"

"What do you mean?"

"Is it mere coincidence that he came to my hometown? I've wondered ever since I got the call about the first victim in Natchez. This is my hometown, and each letter he's sent has gotten more and more personal."

Tory reached across and took Matt's hand, and he appreciated the softness of it against his skin. "You're thinking about your parents?"

He'd phoned his parents on the plane ride into town to warn them to be alert for anything suspicious, but he'd hesitated about actually visiting once he'd arrived, afraid that doing so might lead a killer right to his parents' home. If the killer who'd been one step ahead of him for over a year hadn't found their house already.

Tory stood, reaching out a hand. "Let's go."

"Where?"

"To check on your folks. They'd love to visit with you for a bit."

He was glad for the excuse to go, and called to inform his parents that he was coming for a visit. He and Tory took his SUV, and it was surreal driving back to his childhood home. His parents lived in an upscale neighborhood where they'd been for forty years.

Matt's father had been an insurance salesman for forty years, and his mother was a retired schoolteacher. Neither had understood his drive to join the FBI, as they preferred a simple life of staying home, attending church, and spending time with friends and family. Matt's sister had made them grandparents several years before, and he knew they doted on her kids.

His life had turned out very differently, but he still cared deeply for his mom, dad, and sister. He treasured his family, even if he didn't get to see them as often as he would have liked, due to the demands of his job. And even though they didn't understand his career choice, they had always supported him and his decisions.

Matt parked, and he and Tory got out of the SUV. His father greeted them at the door, shaking his son's hand before pulling him into a bear hug. Matt hugged him back, thankful to sense no animosity over his lack of visits. The last time they'd been together had been at Christmas, three years ago, when he'd taken them all on a holiday cruise. His mom had once assured him that while they would have loved to see him more often, they never wanted to spoil any time they did have with him by being bitter about what they didn't have.

"Tory, it's good to see you again," his dad said, stepping away from Matt to give her a hug.

She returned the greeting warmly. "It's good to see you too, Mr. Shepherd."

Matt's mother appeared from the kitchen, and they repeated the hugs and greetings with her before settling down at the kitchen table, where his mom served homemade pie and sweet tea. It smelled as heavenly as he remembered it.

"Tory, how is your mom?" his mother asked as she loaded a plate.

"She's doing well," Tory replied.

"Is she still living in Shreveport with her sister?"

"She is. I don't imagine she'll be returning to Natchez. Mom says it doesn't feel like home anymore since my dad passed away."

The words hit Matt like a punch to the gut. *Mr. Mills died?*

His face burned with shame that he hadn't been aware, even as his heart twinged with grief. He'd liked Tory's dad. "I'm so sorry, Tory. When did that happen?"

"Four years ago. Heart attack on the golf course." She swallowed hard and tried to force a smile. "At least he died doing what he loved."

"I didn't know," Matt explained softly. "I'm sorry. He was a good man."

Her eyes made it clear that her pain was still raw, and he felt ashamed of not spending more time with his own parents while he still had them.

"Thank you," Tory said. Then she changed the subject and fawned over his mother's apple pie. "I've missed your pie, Mrs. Shepherd."

"Thank you. Dig in, dig in," she instructed them both.

Everyone ate in silence until his father cleaned his plate, wiped his mouth, and sat back in his seat. His voice grew serious as he addressed Matt. "We can guess why you're in town. Liddy Martin?"

Matt nodded, unsurprised his father had pieced it together. He watched the news religiously and would have heard about the murder.

"We attend church with her parents. It's tragic," his mom said. "I'm glad you're on the case, Matt. You too, Tory. You two always worked well together."

Matt couldn't help his smile at the unexpected sentiment. "When did we ever work together, Mom?" They'd been best friends and more but had never worked at the same place.

"At the church's fall bazaar. Don't you remember? You and Tory manned the face-painting booth one year, and so many people told me what a good job you both did. Everyone said your face painting was excellent, and all the kids were walking around with ghosts or pumpkins on their cheeks."

He smiled at the memory as he glanced over at Tory, who also had a grin on her face. He'd forgotten about that. She'd been detail-oriented even then, and her pumpkins had put his ghost paintings to shame.

"I'm sure I could think of a hundred other examples, Matthew. That one came to mind because the church is already planning for the fall harvest carnival and I think about that every year—how proud everyone was of you both, and how happy the kids were that year. The next year, Timothy Spellman and Janice Morgan manned the booth, but they weren't quite as good."

Matt chuckled at his mother's view of his accomplishments.

He'd had many successful years in the FBI, but his greatest success, at least to his mother, had happened over fifteen years before at a church festival.

His mom told more stories of his and Tory's exploits, and a few about Matt while he was growing up. They were good memories, and Matt chuckled as they reminisced. He'd had a good childhood in Natchez. He watched Tory, mesmerized by the sound of her laughter. It was the first time he'd seen her guard down since he'd returned, and it was nice to spend a few hours away from a grim, frustrating case and enjoying nostalgia.

They finally declined more pie and said their goodbyes, with Matt promising to stop by again before he left town.

As they walked back to the SUV, he took Tory's hand and found himself smiling.

"I like your parents," Tory said as they climbed into the SUV. "They're fun. And I loved the photos of your nieces and nephews. Your sister and her husband must have their hands full."

"They really do." He'd enjoyed seeing his parents too, and hoped he would have time to visit his sister once the case ended, assuming they captured the killer. If they didn't, Matt would be off to the next place, chasing after him.

She smiled at him. "You're blessed that your family is still around."

He felt his face warm again at that comment, and he twisted in his seat to face her. "Tory, I'm sorry I didn't know about your father's death."

"How would you have known, Matt?" she asked, an edge to her tone. Her next words were softer. "It's okay. It's been hard. Being an only child, I was always close to my mom and dad, but I have good friends and I'm fortunate to still have Mom. She went to stay with her sister a few months after he died and never came back. I think it's too hard for her to be here without him. She's happier where she is, and we're still really close."

"It's not hard for you?"

"It is, but this is my home. I actually feel closer to my dad here. It comforts me to be in the town where he lived his entire life, getting coffee where he got coffee, shopping where he shopped. I guess that, for my mom, it's too much of a painful reminder of what she's lost."

"So you've never thought about leaving Natchez?"

She shrugged again. "I mean, I've considered it once or twice, but I haven't found anything yet that could pull me away."

Not even me.

The words nearly slipped through his lips, but he choked them back. She'd been right not to follow him. His job kept him traveling more than he was home. It would have gone how she'd predicted when she'd chosen to stay. He would have taken her from a home she loved to a place where she knew no one and he was gone all the time.

He couldn't blame her for choosing the best path for herself.

But it didn't make that decision hurt any less.

Her cell phone buzzed, and her face fell at what she saw on the screen.

"What is it?"

"A hiker has gone missing near the Emerald Mound." She bit her lip. "A female hiker."

His gut churned as he put on his seat belt and started the engine, praying the missing hiker wasn't the second victim.

The killer was wasting no time.

9

*M*att parked in the lot at Emerald Mound, the second largest Native American ceremonial mound in the United States, which covered approximately eight acres and included several smaller mounds. As with most things along the Trace, it was surrounded by wooded areas.

Tory spotted ranger vehicles, Natchez PD, and search-and-rescue vehicles already there.

Chris had called in everyone to assist in finding the hiker. While it didn't necessarily have anything to do with the serial killer on the loose on the Trace—they'd safely located a lost hiker a few months before—it made her feel better knowing local law enforcement was taking the task seriously.

She hopped out of the SUV and hurried over to where Chris was setting up a command post. "I got your text. What happened?"

His expression was grim. "The sheriff's office received this call an hour ago." He pressed play on his cell phone and a recording of a 911 operator came on, followed by a woman whose voice was filled with panic.

"I was hiking in the woods and I got turned around. I can't tell where I am. Please help—"

Chris ended the recording. "The line goes dead after that. The dispatcher tried to call her back, but it went straight to voice mail. According to the number, her name is Jessica Wallace. Rangers located her car here, so this is where we'll start."

"Can they get a trace off her cell phone?" Matt asked.

"No. The battery must have died. It's not giving off any readings."

Out of the corner of her eye, Tory saw tension in Matt's shoulders. Of all the people gathered, only a handful aside from Tory, Matt, and Chris understood that the dropped call might indicate more than a drained cell phone battery.

Chris produced a map. "Let's break up into groups and start a grid search."

"I'll lead a group," Tory offered.

"Me too," Matt said. He slid off his suit coat and she was glad to see him pitching in to help, even if the task might not be related to the serial killer.

Chris gathered up others to lead the teams while Matt pulled Tory aside.

"Be careful out there," he warned. "I asked Chris to place our grids in the same area, so if you find something, I'll be close by."

Tory understood his concern, but she had a duty to help find the missing woman, whether she was a victim of the serial killer or not. There were miles and miles of woods to comb. Hopefully, they could find the hiker before dark.

News about the vanished hiker had spread throughout the community, and by the time they were ready to begin, a group of civilians had arrived to assist. Tory gathered up an equipment pouch—which included a radio, flashlight, water, snacks, and other supplies—then met up with the group that had been assigned to her. It consisted of five individuals, including a face she recognized—Alton Banks, the witness who'd found Liddy Martin's body.

She shook his hand. "Mr. Banks, it's good to see you again. Thank you for volunteering here today."

"Glad to help, Ranger Mills. I like to be of assistance if I can."

Plus I can make my way around the woods pretty well. It's not the first search and rescue I've aided in."

She thanked the others as well, then gave a quick set of instructions for them to follow before they headed out. The most important rule was that she was in charge and they were to remain close to her. She mapped out their grid, then grabbed flashlights in case they were still at work when the sun set, as well as plenty of water.

"Let's go," Tory said, leading the way into the woods. She spotted Matt and a group of others doing the same thing, headed in a different direction.

She did her best to keep her mind on the task at hand, but her thoughts kept returning to the afternoon she'd spent with Matt and his parents.

The few hours had felt like old times, when she and Matt were young, and so much in love. She'd seen his parents around town and at church, and had spoken with them a few times, but it had never been the same after Matt left for Quantico.

It especially struck her how much they loved their grandchildren. Her own children, assuming she ever had any, would never know Tory's father—their grandfather—and that saddened her. As a young adult, she'd always assumed she and Matt would get married one day. It had seemed like an unspoken promise between them, and it hit her again how much she'd lost when he'd left Natchez.

"Ranger Mills?"

She stopped and faced Mr. Banks, who had caught up with her while the others had spread out. She couldn't believe she'd gotten so lost in her thoughts that she hadn't even noticed his presence. She probably wasn't being very thorough if she'd missed an unhidden human's presence. "Yes? What is it?"

"What do you make of that?"

She followed his gaze to a clearing a few yards away, where a man sat beside a rough firepit near a tent.

Illegal camper? Or worse?

"Wait here," she instructed Mr. Banks, as she took her gun from her hip holster and pushed through the brush toward the clearing as quietly as possible.

The man didn't move as she approached. She scanned the clearing for any sign of the missing woman but saw nothing to convince her that anyone else was there.

Though it was possible the missing hiker could be inside the tent.

"National Park Ranger. Don't move," she ordered him.

The man jumped to his feet, raising his hands in the air. "I don't want any trouble." He was tall, thin, and trembling.

"Good. Neither do I," Tory responded. "Is there anyone else around? Anyone inside the tent?"

"No. I'm alone."

"Camping on the Trace is restricted to designated areas. What's your name, sir?"

"Carlton."

"Show me some identification, please, Carlton."

Tory held her breath as he reached into his pocket. If he pulled out anything other than his wallet, they were going to have a problem.

The man inched closer and handed over his driver's license.

Glancing down at the ID, Tory took her gaze off Carlton for a split second—but that was enough.

Something struck her head, hard.

Pain lanced through her, and she collapsed to her knees. Someone who sounded like her seemed to be screaming from far away. The world spun and tilted, and Tory wasn't certain whether she was upright or had fallen prone.

The last thing she saw was Carlton sprinting off into the woods. Then darkness hauled her under.

10

A scream echoed through the woods, stopping Matt in his tracks. He spun around. The civilians in his group appeared as stunned by the noise as he was.

The sound had come from the east—the grid Tory was exploring.

"Wait here," he told his group. He unholstered his gun and plunged into the woods.

He heard shouts for help and finally burst through a clearing, where he spotted several individuals he recognized from Tory's group, huddled together.

One girl ran toward Matt. "Ranger Mills is hurt!"

Matt's heart plummeted into his stomach as he scanned the area, then sprinted toward her. Tory lay unmoving on the ground. He holstered his gun and knelt beside her. Blood trickled from a gash on the side of her head, and a bloody rock sat nearby. He felt for a pulse, breathing more easily when he found one.

"What happened?" he demanded of the group.

The girl who'd approached him answered. "We were covering this area when we heard a scream. By the time we got here, Ranger Mills was on the ground and Mr. Banks was standing over her."

His gaze darted to Banks, who hurried to explain.

"We came across a man who was camping illegally. Ranger Mills told me to wait as she approached him. I heard them exchange words," Alton said. "He picked up the rock and hit her, knocking her to the ground.

The man must not have seen me because when I called out for him to stop, he took off into the woods. I think he was trying to pick her up and take her, which is why I yelled."

"You didn't call for help?" Matt asked, eyes narrowed at Alton Banks.

"Ranger Mills had the radio on her. We were about to make the call when you came from the clearing."

Matt took out his radio and called the command center. "This is Agent Shepherd of the FBI. We have a ranger down."

Ranger Chris Moore responded right away. "What happened?"

"It's Tory. She was hit with a rock. She's unconscious. We need paramedics. And alert the other teams of an assailant." He glanced at Banks for a description.

"Five-nine, slim, blond hair," the other man said.

Matt relayed the description.

"I've got two EMTs on the way, along with a couple of crime scene techs," Moore said. "Everyone else is still out searching for the missing hiker."

Matt selected the woman who had approached him about Tory's injury, along with another man. "Go watch for the EMTs and lead them here."

The pair hurried off. Tory was still unconscious. She must have been hit hard. Blood ran down the side of her neck.

Mr. Banks handed Matt a towel. "Here, you can use this to stop the bleeding."

Matt took the towel and thanked Banks, then pressed it against Tory's wound.

Great. He had a civilian telling him how to handle an injured person. That was how rattled he was.

"Tell me more about this camper," he said, trying to recover some of his faculties.

Could Tory's assailant be the serial killer? Or a random person looking to lie low in the woods along the Natchez Trace Parkway?

Banks went through everything about the camper again, but it wasn't much despite Matt's questions, though they were designed to jog a witness's memory.

The EMTs arrived and rushed to treat Tory. Matt moved away, allowing space for them to take care of her. Seeing her unconscious on the ground had shocked him, and he found that the thought of losing her was something he couldn't wrap his mind around. But he couldn't allow his focus to change. He hadn't returned to Natchez to reignite a lost love. He was there to capture a serial killer and save lives.

Tory moaned as they loaded her onto a gurney and then to the back of an all-terrain vehicle.

Matt ran to her side. "Tory, are you okay?"

Her eyes fluttered as she groaned again. "Wh—what happened?"

"You were attacked."

Understanding dawned in her eyes. "The camper."

"Did you see him?"

"I spoke to him. He was camping out here like you said, Matt."

The idea that the killer was living off the land might be true after all.

"What about the missing hiker? Did you see any signs of her?"

"No. I only saw him. He handed me his identification. I dropped it when I fell."

"I'll find it. Don't worry."

Every fiber of his being screamed at him to go with Tory as they loaded her into the ambulance, but he stopped himself. He had to focus on the job and on determining whether or not Tory's assailant was, in fact, their killer. If he was, they had to set up a perimeter.

But they couldn't use civilians to do so. They would have to change the setup from search and rescue for a missing hiker to a hunt for a killer.

He sent the civilians with the EMTs and walked around the campsite with the crime scene techs. He spotted the driver's license near where Tory had been found.

He placed it into an evidence bag before studying it. The name on the identification was Dennis Carlton.

"Who are you, Dennis Carlton?" Matt snapped a photo of the identification and forwarded it to Ranger Moore before phoning him.

"How's Tory?" Chris Moore asked in lieu of a greeting.

"She's alive," Matt said. "She got hit on the head, but she'll be fine. The EMTs are bringing her in now. Witnesses said the man who attacked her was trying to grab her. He ran off into the woods when he saw the group approaching. We might need to change our tactics since he's out here. If we find him, we might find the missing hiker too."

"Well, actually, I've received notification that the hiker was found. She got turned around on the trail and her phone battery died. I hate to break it to you, but this had nothing to do with the killer you're hunting."

Matt's head spun. It was possible that the killer had taken advantage of the operation in order to target Tory. Matt was thankful they didn't have a second deceased victim yet, but he didn't like what the new situation seemed to indicate. Had the killer been sitting out there, ready to strike whoever came upon him? Or was he targeting Tory specifically?

Matt cleared his throat before speaking, working to keep the flood of emotions from his voice. "Can you arrange to have a team meet me here to help the techs process the campsite? It's possible we might be able to recover evidence. I also want to use those helicopters to search for our assailant, now that the hiker has been found."

Carlton couldn't have gotten very far on foot, especially not with so many people already combing the woods for him.

"I'll arrange it," Chris said, "but it might take time to change the parameters. They're bringing Tory in now. I'll get back to you."

He pictured Chris hurrying toward Tory to make certain she was okay, and Matt couldn't help but feel a little envious. Chris would get the privilege of taking care of Tory, instead of Matt.

But surely that was for the best. Once the job was finished, Matt would head back to Quantico, and she would remain in Natchez. Nothing had changed between them, so it didn't matter that he was as drawn to her as he'd been in high school, when they'd been kids in love.

But that love hadn't been stronger than his ambition, which he regretted. He had a good career, one he was proud of, but it had cost him greatly.

Seeing Tory lying there on the ground had awakened a new fear inside of him—the fear of losing her for good.

He was no longer certain the cost of his career had been worth it.

How embarrassing.

Tory leaned back against the hospital bed and tried to replay the events of the attack in her mind. She hadn't even seen it coming. How Dennis Carlton had the time to grab a rock and hit her with it was simply baffling. Yet she couldn't deny the gash on her head or the fact that she'd been unconscious for what felt like ages.

The emergency room doctor wanted to admit her due to her loss of consciousness, but Tory felt fine except for a little soreness and a headache. She was ready to get out of there and get back to work.

Hopefully, the new development wouldn't convince Matt to drop her from his team.

Funny—when he'd first requested that she join his team, she hadn't wanted to work with him. One short day later, she didn't want to lose the opportunity. She was determined to capture the killer and get him off the streets of her town before he hurt anyone else.

Someone knocked on the door to her room and Chris entered, carrying a bunch of colorful flowers. She pasted on a smile and tried to shove down the feeling of disappointment that it wasn't Matt standing in her doorway.

"They're beautiful," she said as Chris handed her the bouquet. "Thank you."

"They're from all of us at the ranger station. I'm supposed to bring back a report on how you're doing."

"I'm fine, Chris. Truly. I'm ready to get out of here and get back to work."

"Tory, you were attacked. I think you can take a day or two to recover."

"I'm fine." At that moment, a sharp pain shot through her head. She winced and pressed her hand against her brow to quell it. "I *will* be fine," she corrected herself. "It's nothing a few painkillers won't take care of."

She didn't like her boss's worried expression, and she anticipated seeing it mirrored on the faces of her coworkers and colleagues. It made her feel helpless, and that was the last thing she wanted her colleagues to think.

"I can't figure out how he got the better of me, Chris. I was being so careful."

"The witnesses in your group said he hit you when you looked away."

"I glanced at his driver's license maybe a second. I don't understand how he got the upper hand so fast."

"I spoke with the witnesses myself." Chris flipped open a notebook and consulted the scribbles inside. "Mr. Alton Banks said he witnessed the whole thing. He thought the attacker already had the rock ready in his hand."

That can't be right, Tory thought, second-guessing the sequence of events. "I'm sure his hands were empty. He raised them when I approached."

"Could be you're remembering it wrong, or your memory has been affected by the attack," Chris suggested.

But Tory was certain she had a clear memory of what had happened. Or she thought she had.

"Tory, I don't have to remind you that you aren't the first law enforcement officer to be attacked. It happens sometimes, even if we've done everything right. You were lucky Mr. Banks was there.

That camper apparently tried to drag you into the woods. Who knows what he would have done to you if that had happened?" Her boss's expression held a mix of distress and relief.

She shuddered at the idea. If Dennis Carlton was indeed the serial killer Matt hunted, then Alton Banks had saved her life. "I suppose I owe Mr. Banks a big thank-you," she said, shaking her head.

"He's had an eventful couple of days," Chris agreed. "First he discovered one woman, then he rescued another. It'll be a vacation he won't soon forget."

Tory chuckled. Chris was probably right. Although it was not the impression she ever wished on anyone who visited her beloved city.

And speaking of people who were visiting her city, she'd been at the hospital for hours and Matt had yet to check on her. She told herself it shouldn't matter, but disappointment flittered through her all the same.

"Agent Shepherd remained at the scene to make sure everything was processed correctly," Chris told her.

She felt her face warm with embarrassment. Were her feelings so obvious?

"He also arranged for a sweep of the area to find the attacker, but we finally ended the search an hour ago without locating him. He must have gone into deep hiding."

Naturally Matt was working the case. That was why he'd come to town after all. Not to see her.

A nurse entered Tory's room. "The doctor has signed your release forms, Ranger Mills."

"That's great news. Thank you"

"He did it reluctantly, noting that you should rest," the nurse added, her mouth a firm, serious line. "You should take it easy once you get home."

"I'll take you home," Chris stated. "You're off the schedule for at least the next few days."

"That's not necessary," Tory protested. "I'm perfectly fine."

"We'll see. Chief Scott is also arranging to have an officer posted at your house for your protection."

"That's crazy."

"Not as crazy as you think. Dennis Carlton tried to abduct you, Tory. Agent Shepherd believes he might be targeting you, and we're not taking any chances. After all, you were in that photo and then you were attacked in the woods. Who's to say Carlton won't return to finish the job?"

It was silly to think that one incident could be blown up into something so significant. She'd stumbled across Carlton in the woods and he'd reacted. The fact that he'd tried to abduct her was irrelevant. He likely would have done so to any woman who'd interrupted his solitude.

But she knew from her interviews with Matt that the serial killer wasn't opportunistic. He stalked and hunted his victims. It was a long shot, but maybe he had somehow arranged for the hiker to go missing and used the opportunity to target Tory.

That still troubled her, even as Chris drove her to her house. The dogs ran out to the truck, barking as she got out. They bounced around with excitement, and she stopped to pet each of them before heading inside.

Chris followed her and made certain she was settled in. "Do you need anything?"

"Only to get back to work." She lowered herself onto the couch, ignoring her achy muscles as she did so.

"I will call you in the morning, and we'll see how you are," he replied firmly. "*Then* we'll talk about putting you back on the schedule."

Although, since you've been working with Agent Shepherd, we won't have to cover much." He went into the kitchen and returned with a cup of ice water, setting it on the end table beside her. "You should stay hydrated," he said when she glared at him.

Her primary focus had been working with Matt rather than covering ranger duties since the discovery of Liddy Martin's body. That meant her absence wouldn't create much of a hole in the ranger schedule, but who could help Matt in her absence? She prayed again that he hadn't changed his mind about wanting her on the task force.

She heard the dogs barking outside again.

Chris peered through the window. "That's a Natchez PD car setting up at the end of your driveway. They'll keep watch."

She hated having such a fuss made over her. She didn't want police protection. Her dogs and her law enforcement training were all the defense she required.

A black SUV parked beside Chris's vehicle in her driveway. She glanced through the window and saw Matt get out. He bent down to pet each dog before heading toward the door. Her heart skipped a beat at the idea that he might see her so disheveled. She gently touched the bandage on her forehead and smoothed her hair.

Chris grinned at her. "I'll let you two visit and call you tomorrow."

Her boss exited the house, stopping momentarily to speak to Matt before climbing into his SUV and driving away.

Matt stood at the door that Chris had left open. "Okay to come in?"

"Yes."

He stepped inside, closing the door behind him. When he took in the sight of her, his jaw tightened. "How are you feeling, Tory?"

"I'm fine, Matt. The doctor said I might have a very mild concussion. I have a headache and some stitches, but I'm okay."

"I'm sorry I didn't get to the hospital to see you."

"It's okay. You had a job to do." Sure, she'd been disappointed that he hadn't dropped everything to see if she was all right, but that was irrational. Hunting a serial killer was more important than a minor bump on her head. "Chris told me that the search didn't produce anything."

Matt grimaced. "This guy went deep into the woods, I guess. I did get some information back from his license, though."

"Yes?"

"It was fake. The name Dennis Carlton was bogus. However, we did manage to get a fingerprint from the license. I had it fast-tracked. It belongs to a man named John Ricks."

"Does he have a criminal history?"

"Oh yes," Matt confirmed. "Armed robbery, assaults, even attempted murder. He has warrants out in three different states. This could finally be the lead that breaks this case, and it's all because of you, Tory."

"I didn't do anything. I stumbled across him in the woods."

"You got the license and the fingerprint," Matt countered.

"Chris said you think he might be targeting me. Why would he do that?"

"I mentioned that the killer has made this case personal with me, Tory. You were in that photograph with me. Now he's attacked you in the woods. It's too many occurrences for me to believe it's merely coincidence, so we should take precautions. The smart thing would be to take you off the case."

Her stomach sank as he said the words she'd feared. "But there's no way Dennis—I mean, John Ricks could have predicted that I would be there, Matt. It was dumb luck that we came across him. He had nothing to do with the missing hiker. I don't see how this makes me a target."

He rubbed his face. "What's wrong with being cautious?"

"It makes me look weak," she snapped. "Like I can't handle myself and have to be fussed over. Once you're gone, I still have to work with these people. I don't want my coworkers or Natchez PD or the sheriff's office thinking I can't do my job."

"Tory, no one could think that after your ten years of success as a law enforcement ranger. But you were brutally attacked. You must take time to recover. That's all."

"And you made that decision without checking with me."

"I would have done the same for anyone."

She stared up into his eyes. "Would you, Matt?" She doubted it. She was a trained and skilled law enforcement ranger. She didn't want anyone, especially her ex-boyfriend, to see her as someone who couldn't protect herself.

Not that I did such a great job of that earlier today.

His cheeks reddened and he gave up the pretense. "Okay, maybe I wouldn't have done it for anyone, but you're not just anyone, are you, Tory? This killer has made this quest personal, and I don't want you paying for something that has more to do with me than with you. He's come to my hometown. Now you're on his radar because of your association with me. I have to make certain he's not targeting you on my account, and keep you safe if that's what he is doing."

She studied the full image of Matt Shepherd. He'd been little more than a boy when he'd left, and had returned a grown man with a successful career. She couldn't deny she still found him attractive and was flattered that he was worried about her, but their lives were very different. He would leave Natchez once the killer was caught, and she would be left behind again. She couldn't allow his presence to have a negative effect on her career or her life.

She lifted her chin. "I have a job, Matt, and I'm good at it. I don't need someone from the FBI undermining that in front of my colleagues, no matter what your intentions are. I can take care of myself. I have to in order to keep faith with my colleagues."

He straightened, smoothing out his suit jacket. "I understand. I'm sorry, Tory. I told myself I could keep a professional attitude around you, but I was obviously wrong. If you'd like to distance yourself from this case, I can request someone else as my liaison."

That wasn't what she wanted either. Tears filled her eyes. She twisted away from him and took a drink of water from the cup Chris had brought for her, blinking them back. "I'm committed to finding this killer. I want you to treat me like you would anyone else you were working with."

When her emotions were under control, she faced him again to find he had stepped closer. His eyes bore into hers before he moved his hand to gently touch her bandaged head.

His fingers brushed her cheek, and he shook his head. "I'm not sure that's something I'd ever be able to do, Tory, because you'll never be just anyone else." He walked out the door.

Through the window, she watched his SUV pull away, her heart hammering from the mere touch of his hand.

12

$\mathcal{M}$att slammed his palm against the steering wheel as he drove. He hadn't meant for things to get so personal between him and Tory. He'd really thought he could keep his emotional distance from her while working the case.

What an idiot I was to ever believe that.

He'd known the moment he saw her lying on the ground that emotional distance was something he would never be able to maintain.

He would have to do better if he wanted her help. It was invaluable, but he was no longer sure about dragging her into his nightmare and putting her life at risk.

Not that he would be able to keep her away. She'd told him she wasn't backing down. The killer had made it personal with Matt, and then he'd made it personal with Tory by killing in her hometown.

Matt drove to his hotel room. He could have stayed with his parents, but keeping his distance from them was important if he didn't want to put them in harm's way too. He'd felt better after he and Tory had gone to see them, but he didn't want to place a target on their backs.

He showered, changed, then dropped into bed. He clicked on the TV and let the noise play in the background as he went over his notes for at least the millionth time. He'd sent out a BOLO for John Ricks with the rangers, local police, and even Mississippi and Louisiana state patrols. But finding Ricks wouldn't be enough. Matt had to be able to connect Ricks to the areas where the other murders had occurred if he wanted to prove that Ricks was the serial killer they were searching for.

Matt brought up Ricks's extensive criminal history. He had a history of violence and had been a suspect in a previous attempted murder a few years back. A bad guy, most likely, but was he Matt's bad guy?

He dug through the file, hoping to find some charges that matched the areas where the other murders had occurred. He didn't find any that were anywhere close to the national parks where the other murders were committed. That could mean that Ricks simply hadn't been caught committing crimes in any of those spots.

Or he wasn't their killer.

In the morning, Matt would contact the local law enforcement agencies where the other murders had occurred and share John Ricks's information to see if any of them recognized the suspect. Perhaps there was something on their radar that hadn't shown up on Ricks's official rap sheet.

Matt's cell phone rang and he glanced at the screen—Agent Vivian Ferguson of the ISB. She'd been the one to bring him into the serial killer investigation but had stayed behind in Great Smoky Mountains National Park when they'd gotten the call about the Natchez murder.

He hit the answer key. "Hi, Vivian. Any updates?"

She sounded as tired and frustrated as he felt. "Nothing. We closed out the scene, but so far we haven't found any additional evidence that might help identify our suspect. I'll be heading to Natchez in a few days to assist you there. I hope you're having better luck than I am."

"How about I tell you what's been happening, and you tell me if it's better?" He spoke to Vivian for several minutes, going over everything they'd dealt with so far, including the day's attack on Tory.

"Let's hope you're able to tie Ricks to the other murders," Vivian said. "Then all we have to do is locate him again."

"Actually, he's quite adept at hiding out," Matt responded. "After he attacked Tory, we found out he was using a fake ID. It was only through the fingerprints on it that we uncovered his true identity. He's got warrants in several states once we do bring him in." He got up and paced to the window, gazing at the bridge lit up over the Mississippi River. "In the meantime, we're twiddling our thumbs while he might be out stalking his next victim, and there's nothing we can do."

"There's always something, Matt."

He enjoyed working with Vivian and found her to be a capable investigator. They'd become friends since he'd first been called in to work the serial killer case eighteen months before.

He'd come to understand her pretty well, so he could sense when her conversation was about to change direction.

"Since you have some downtime on this case, I wonder if you'd be willing to help me with something else," she said, her tone slightly awkward.

"Another case, Viv? I haven't solved this one yet." He was surprised that she was working on something else. He knew the ISB agents had a lot to handle and didn't have nearly as many hands available as the FBI, but a serial killer case should take top priority.

"I know, I know. One of the rangers here dropped this one on me out of the blue. I need another set of eyes and maybe a preliminary profile. I'm not sure if there's anything here that warrants a full-blown investigation or not, but they're really pushing for one."

"What's the case?"

"A fifty-six-year-old woman named Delores Taylor fell off a cliff here at Great Smoky Mountains National Park. Her husband claims she was taking photos of birds and stumbled, falling over the side of a rock cliff. At first, it appeared accidental, but the rangers must investigate every death. It was determined that the guardrail should have prevented a fall, which raised a red flag. Also, apparently, witnesses overheard the couple arguing the night before her fall.

The rangers investigated the husband, Henry Taylor, but there was nothing concrete to charge him on. There doesn't seem to be much of a motive either. Mrs. Taylor had no big life insurance policy, and there was little money in the couple's joint bank account, so they don't think it was financially motivated."

"What do they think?"

"I can't tell, but they are determined that this was no accident. We could use another set of eyes to figure out which direction to go, or if it even warrants another look. Are you willing to go over the file?"

He rubbed his eyes. He wouldn't mind getting his head out of the serial case for a while, at least until something new broke. "Sure, go ahead and email it to me. I'll review it and get back to you."

His phone dinged, indicating a text was coming through. He glanced at the screen. It was good news from Chief Scott. "I have to go, Vivian. Natchez PD has located Victor Lance's white pickup at the casino. I'll get back to you with whatever I figure out about your file, okay?"

"No problem. Thanks, Matt."

He ended the call, then dressed quickly and hopped back into his SUV. It was a good thing he'd stayed close to downtown instead of in the suburbs at his parents' house. He was pulling into the casino parking lot within five minutes.

Police vehicle lights lit up the night. Matt flashed his credentials to an officer directing traffic, who waved him through. After parking, Matt hurried to where he spotted crime scene tape surrounding a white pickup. The doors to the truck were open, and crime scene techs collected evidence inside and out.

He spotted Sheriff Ford and Chief Scott and approached them. "What have you found?"

Chief Scott responded, "Patrols located the pickup here. We're having the security team search their video feeds. So far, we've found no sign of Lance."

Disappointed, Matt stared at the truck. He'd been so focused on John Ricks that he'd let Victor Lance fall under the radar.

"We're not giving up," Sheriff Ford stated. "We've got patrols setting up roadblocks in and out of the city. I also contacted Ranger Moore to watch for activity on the Trace."

"The original BOLO is still in place, right?" Matt asked. That meant all local law enforcement should already be watching for the truck.

"Right, but now that we have the truck in our possession, we'll update it to reflect that. If he's abandoned this vehicle, we have no idea what he might be driving—if he's driving anything."

"My team will get the truck processed and let you know what we find," Chief Scott assured him.

"Thanks. You said you talked to casino security. Did their cameras capture Lance when he arrived? Did they see him get out of the pickup?"

"Yes," Scott confirmed. "They have him on camera. In fact, they're the ones who called us when they spotted it. The footage shows him entering the casino, but he eventually slipped out of view."

Matt studied the casino, which overlooked the Mississippi River and had been built in such a way that the exterior resembled an old sawmill. "Let's canvass inside, and outside the casino as well. Maybe Lance is still somewhere on the premises. If we have him on video entering the building, he either got out some way without being seen, or else he's still here somewhere."

"I'll gather some officers to assist you," Scott offered.

"Thank you, Chief."

"Matt?"

He whirled around to find Tory hurrying toward them. It was odd to see her in jeans and a T-shirt rather than her normal ranger uniform—actually, it was odd to see her there at all. The big white bandage on her head was a visible reminder that she should have been at home in bed. "What are you doing here? You should be resting."

"I heard on the police scanner that the truck was found. Did you find Lance?"

Sheriff Ford shook his head. "Only the truck so far."

"We're about to start a canvass," Matt added.

"I'll help with that," Tory said.

He was glad she felt up to that, but he worried she would overdo it and set back her recovery. Not that he could refuse her. She'd made it perfectly clear earlier that she was in charge of her own decisions and didn't want him treating her with kid gloves, especially in front of others in the law enforcement community. He didn't like the situation, but he could stay with her to monitor how she felt, whether she wanted him to or not. "Okay. Tory and I will head inside with the other officers. Give us a shout if you find anything in the truck or outside."

They stepped through the casino entrance and were met with loud music, slot machine sounds, and the murmur of a crowd. The casino was bustling on the hot summer night. The place had not been there when Matt had left Natchez. They'd built it to blend in with the city's historic atmosphere, but inside it was exactly what one would expect from a casino.

They spread out to speak with dealers, players, and staff, flashing Lance's photo for everyone to see. They found no one who recognized him or could place him inside the casino, although Matt knew most people were too focused on their own activities to pay much attention to people coming and going around them.

Finally, Matt dismissed the officers. He and Tory made their way to the security room to review the videos for themselves, in case they managed to catch something new.

The security chief on duty showed them the footage of the truck rolling into the parking lot. Matt's pulse quickened when he spotted a man get out and walk into the casino. It was definitely Victor Lance, the man witnesses had seen fleeing from Liddy Martin's crime scene. No doubt about it. They switched to another camera, which captured him walking through the main floor, then disappearing into a bathroom. He never came back out.

"And that bathroom was searched?" Matt asked the security officer.

"It was, by us and by the police. There was no way for him to get out of there without being seen, but somehow he pulled it off. If he got out of the casino, he could have gone down by the bluffs and out of camera range."

"I want to go over it ourselves and see if we can figure out how Lance managed to escape," Matt told Tory.

She agreed, and they walked back down to the casino floor. Matt entered the men's room and called out to make sure no one else was inside before motioning Tory in. The room had no exterior windows through which Lance could have climbed to escape. So how had he sneaked past the security videos? Matt and Tory checked all the other rooms they could find that someone might hide in, but there was no sign of Lance or any clue as to where he might have gone.

Tory opened a door that let them out of the casino. A wooden staircase led down to sidewalks that paralleled the river, as the security officer had stated.

Matt peered around and didn't see any video cameras. "It's possible he got out this way and walked down the bluffs."

"Lance must be aware that we're looking for him if he's making an effort to hide from the cameras," Tory observed.

"But how?" Matt wondered aloud. "There's been no activity on his cell phone, and he hasn't called his wife. We've been monitoring her line."

"Then she must have contacted him by some other means." Tory stopped and sat on one of the benches along the sidewalk. "Maybe he has a friend he would go to and his wife wasn't being truthful with us."

Matt shook his head and took the spot beside her. Tory had a point. If Mrs. Lance had contacted her husband on a friend's phone, they wouldn't know, but someone must have tipped him off about the police manhunt for him.

"This guy is smart, Tory. Why would he allow his pickup to be found here and the cameras to capture him going inside? Is he toying with us?"

"He does seem to like games, doesn't he?"

Matt rubbed his face as he gazed out at the lights of the bridge that gleamed against the night sky over the river. He remembered being down there before there were sidewalks and benches and streetlights, when the cool breeze off the water and quiet privacy were the area's main attractions. Now, there was a casino where anyone could spend money, have a nice buffet meal, and stare out at the water. "This place is nothing like I imagined when my mom told me they were building it," he said, gesturing to the casino.

It was one of many things that had changed since he'd been gone.

Tory took a deep breath, then asked softly, "Why didn't you ever come home, Matt?"

Her question surprised him, and he gaped at her.

She rushed to clarify. "I mean, I get why you left, but you still have family here. Your mom and dad, your sister. Fifteen years is a long time not to visit. Christmases, birthdays, anniversaries—you missed them all. Why? What kept you away?"

It wasn't as if he hadn't seen his family in all that time. He'd paid for his parents and sister's family to come visit him. He'd met them at resorts and vacation spots, but Tory was right. He hadn't set foot back in Natchez in years.

He'd tried not to think about it. He'd made plane reservations back home many times, only to cancel and change his plans.

And there was one reason why.

"You." The truth slipped from his lips before he could stop it.

Tory's eyes widened, then she ducked her head to examine her hands, twisting in her lap. He'd embarrassed her, though he hadn't meant to.

The truth was out. He might as well finish his confession.

"I never stopped thinking about you, Tory. I guess I always knew that if I came back to Natchez and saw you again, I might start rethinking why I left in the first place. Everything I worked to build would have been lost."

Ironically, that was exactly what was happening anyway. Ever since he'd seen her that first day, things had been different. He'd been feeling restless, and it had less to do with the case than it did with Tory.

"I never meant to put you in that kind of position, Matt," she said, her voice laced with regret. "You could have come and gone without seeing me. I would have understood."

"I don't think that's true. In fact, now that I'm back, I'm certain it isn't. When I first received the call about a body found in Natchez, matching the other serial victims, my first thought wasn't that the killer had moved on. It was that I might see you again. I finally had a reason to return that had nothing to do with my feelings, but it was still an excuse to indulge in those feelings, even though I foolishly thought

I could control them. After all, I spend my life compartmentalizing. I push my own thoughts aside to investigate cases. I intentionally don't focus on the horror of what I see every single day so that I can be objective. I thought I could put you and what we used to have in a box so that I could work this case, but I was wrong. I should have stayed away altogether."

She looked up at him with tears in her eyes. "I don't know what to say, Matt."

"There's nothing for you to say, Tory."

"I can't deny that those feelings are still there for me too, but nothing in our lives has changed. You're still off living your FBI dream, and I'm still here—a homebody who loves this place. I don't see how we could ever get past that without one of us giving up a piece of ourselves, and I don't want that."

It hurt him to realize she was right. Nothing had changed. They were still struggling to climb that same old hurdle that had kept them apart for so many years. "I'm sorry too." He pushed himself to his feet. "I'll take you home. You must be tired."

"I have my own vehicle," Tory said, resignation in her voice. "A couple of the rangers dropped it off for me after you left my place earlier."

"Then I'll walk you back up to it."

They climbed back up the bluff to the casino parking lot, which was slowly beginning to clear out as the activity inside wound down.

Matt walked Tory to her car, made sure she was safely inside, then watched as she drove away, reflecting on whether he'd done the right thing by being honest with her. On one hand, it felt good to have gotten on the same page as her.

On the other hand, when that page meant they agreed that they could never be together, he was more miserable than ever.

13

"*I* heard about the excitement last night," Chris said when Tory called him the next day.

She'd been out late with Matt at the casino and was as disappointed as he'd been that they hadn't caught Victor Lance. The man apparently had a knack for staying under the radar.

"I also heard you were right there in the middle of it," Chris continued, his tone mildly reproachful.

She was glad they were on the phone so he couldn't see her face redden. "I heard the report on the scanner and wanted to see what was happening. Matt wasn't happy to see me there either."

"I'm glad he didn't let you overdo it, Tory. You're too determined for your own good."

She knew Chris was watching out for her best interests, but sometimes he treated her more like a little sister than a fellow officer. "I feel fine," she insisted.

In truth, she was still a little sore and her head ached, but it was nothing a few over-the-counter painkillers couldn't control. She was ready to get back on the job. Sitting around the house was making her edgy. She'd already cleaned every room, rearranged her mantel, and binged several episodes of a true crime show.

As much as she loved her cabin in the woods, she was eager to get back to work.

Chris hesitated. "Are you sure you're up to this? If Matt doesn't think you're ready, maybe you're not."

"He's being overly cautious. When I say I'm fine, I am."

He finally relented. "Okay, you can be on call tonight, but I want you to spend the day resting. And if you find yourself needing help, call for it. Don't try to be a hero, Tory. No one is judging you for recuperating after you were attacked."

"I'll be careful. Thanks, Chris."

She ended the call, glad that her boss had agreed to put her back on the rotation. She was tired of sitting at home, and she didn't want anyone to think she was weak. His comment about not judging her hit a sore spot. She loved her job as a ranger, but she'd had her fair share of local law enforcement who questioned her abilities simply because she was a woman. It always made her even more determined to prove herself to others.

And she certainly didn't want Matt questioning her abilities.

She spent the rest of the afternoon rearranging her bookshelves and treating her lingering headache with cold compresses, before deciding to take a stroll through the woods. One thing she loved about her cabin was the vast forest behind her house. She soaked in the sunshine, the smell of pine, and the crunch of sticks and leaves beneath her feet. Jojo, Bingo, and Bob trotted happily around her, enjoying the walk.

But it was also a hot summer day and the heat soon became stifling, so they headed back. She and the dogs were nearly back to the house when her cell phone buzzed. She glanced at the screen and saw it was her mother calling, which wasn't going to do a thing to help her headache. Tory loved her mom and was thankful to still have her, but her mother was also a chatterbox.

"Tory, I just heard about the murder of that woman on the news," she said when Tory answered the call. "It's terrible. They said she was found on the Trace. Were you involved in that?"

"I was the ranger on duty when the call came in."

"Who killed her? It's always the boyfriend, isn't it? That's what all the crime shows say."

Tory couldn't discuss an open case with her mother, and she was certain her mom didn't really want the details. Besides, telling her about a serial killer would be tantamount to calling the local news station and broadcasting it. Her mom wouldn't be able to keep the news to herself.

"We're still investigating, Mom. There haven't been any arrests yet."

Tory could hear the worry in her mother's tone when she spoke again. "I don't like the idea of you being out there all alone in those woods. It could have been you who came across some crazed maniac."

Loretta Mills hated that her daughter had joined the law enforcement rangers, but she hated even more that Tory wouldn't share details of her cases. Though there was one juicy bit of information Tory could share with her mother.

"You'll never guess who's back in town, Mom. Matt Shepherd."

Her mother gasped. "He is? How does he look?"

Tory laughed. She couldn't lie. "Great." Better than he had a right to, in Tory's opinion. It didn't seem fair that he could leave her, become a big success, then swoop back into town even more attractive than he had been in school.

"Did he call you?"

"We're working a case together."

Her mother sighed. "I imagine he probably has a wife and a houseful of kids by now, doesn't he?"

Tory grimaced. Her mother had always liked Matt and had been nearly as devastated as her daughter when he'd left town. In fact, her mom had never been shy about pointing out how big a mistake she thought it had been for Tory to let him go.

"Actually, he doesn't. He's still single."

Her mother squealed. "Tory, you have to take a chance. You've been pining away for that man all these years."

"I have not been pining," Tory protested.

"Well, you've never dated much. What other explanation is there?"

Tory rolled her eyes. "Mom, I have dated. And the explanation is that my job keeps me very busy."

But her mother was spot on in part of her analysis—Tory had yet to meet a man who measured up to her standards. *Is that because I compare them all to Matt Shepherd?*

The dogs darted ahead of her, and she heard a vehicle approaching as she made her way back to the cabin. "Mom, I have to go. Someone is here." She rounded the back of the house, then smiled when she spotted Matt's SUV pulling up beside her vehicle. "It's him."

He got out and waved, holding up a bag of food. "I brought dinner," he called out. "I hope that's okay."

She met him at his vehicle. "That's lovely. Thank you." She covered the microphone on her cell phone. "I'm talking to my mom."

He grinned. "Tell her I said hi."

But her mother had other plans. "I want to talk to him," she said.

Tory held out the phone to Matt. "Tell her yourself."

Matt took the phone. "Mrs. Mills, hello. It's so nice to speak to you again."

His smile faded, and Tory couldn't stifle a giggle that escaped her lips. She imagined her mother was giving him an earful for leaving her daughter brokenhearted all those years ago. Or she was building Tory up to him. Possibly both.

"Yes ma'am. I promise I'll look after her," he said finally. "Goodbye, Mrs. Mills." He handed back the phone, his expression telling her he'd been through the wringer.

"I'll call you back later, Mom," Tory said when Matt handed back her cell phone. "I'm sorry about that. I thought she wanted to say hi. I didn't realize she was going to give you a piece of her mind."

He smiled. "It's okay. It's nothing I didn't deserve. I broke her daughter's heart. She has a right to read me the riot act over it."

Tory felt her face warm. "That was a long time ago, Matt."

"I know, but moms don't forget." He hefted the bag of food. "I hope you're hungry."

She realized she was starving, and it was nice of him to bring supper. However, she hadn't heard from him all day, and he had been pretty miffed with her showing up at the casino unexpectedly the night before. She hoped the meal wouldn't end in an "It's been great working with you, but..." speech. She wasn't ready to be booted from the case. No matter what else had happened between them, she still needed to get a serial killer off the streets of her town.

She opened the front door to her cabin and ushered him inside, closing the door behind them.

Matt deposited the food onto her kitchen island. "I hope you still like ribs."

She smiled. "I love them." It was a reminder of the days they'd spent together. The fact that he'd remembered her favorite food touched her, but it still didn't answer the big question hanging over them.

Tory helped him unload their meals—her ribs and his barbecue chicken plate, then decided to rip off the bandage. "Did you come here tonight to tell me I'm off the case? That you don't want me to be your liaison with the rangers anymore?"

He leaned across the kitchen island and locked eyes with her. "I don't play games, Tory. I'm glad you're on my side. If you're up to it, I still want you on my team."

"Well, I am up to it. I even had Chris put me back on rotation," she said, even as her heart fluttered at the light scent of his cologne.

"I'm glad to hear it," Matt said, sliding a plate of ribs and potato salad toward her.

"I was worried when I didn't hear from you today," she admitted as she took in the sight of the food, her stomach grumbling—whether with nerves or hunger, it was difficult to tell.

"Well, I figured since there wasn't much to do at that point, you shouldn't have to come in. Besides, you were up pretty late last night. I figured you might want to sleep in."

She noted dark circles under his weary eyes and threw the question back at him. "Did you sleep in?"

He grinned. "No."

They were both the same when it came to doing their jobs—working as hard as possible to do their duty well. No matter the cost to them, neither would allow a killer to endanger the innocent people in their charge for a second longer than they had to.

"We're still searching for the man who attacked you in the woods, while also keeping vigilant regarding Victor Lance," he told her. "I'm also waiting on Lance's driving logs. But I spent most of my day trying to connect John Ricks to any of the other crime scenes. I emailed his photo to several pertinent law enforcement agencies, but so far nothing has clicked into place."

"Then he might not be the serial killer," Tory suggested.

"It's a possibility." Matt bit into a piece of chicken.

"But if that's the case, why attack me?"

"Ricks is a wanted fugitive, and you're law enforcement. Maybe he knew if you arrested him for illegal camping, then his fake identification wouldn't hold up once you ran his prints."

"But not why he tried to drag me into the woods. I mean, with me unconscious, he could have gotten away clean. Kidnapping me would have complicated his problems, not solved them. If Mr. Banks hadn't been there, Ricks might have killed me." She shuddered at the thought of being so helpless, at a killer's mercy. No wonder she was struggling with the idea that her colleagues might view her as being weak.

"We won't know what Ricks intended until we find him and ask. As it stands, we have two reasonable suspects and can't locate either one." Matt wiped his hands on a napkin. "It makes me want to forget it all and concentrate on this other case."

She blinked in surprise, a bite of ribs halfway to her mouth. "You're working another case?" She would have thought all his energy would be going toward catching the serial killer.

"Kind of. Agent Ferguson requested a preliminary profile on a different case." He went over the specifics for Tory, even showing her photographs from where the woman had fallen.

It was an interesting set of circumstances, and Tory was intrigued—as well as flattered that he would share such things with her. "I agree with the park rangers that the guardrail should have prevented her from falling on her own, but with no obvious motive, it sounds like they need to do a deep dive on the rest of the victim's life and find out if there might have been a reason for someone to want her dead."

"Solid assessment. You'd make a good profiler," Matt said with a wink.

She smiled, certain he was just being nice, but it felt good to have his approval. "Actually, Chris keeps telling me I should apply to ISB as a criminal investigator the next time a position opens up."

"That would mean leaving Natchez, wouldn't it?" Matt asked, not meeting her eyes.

"Exactly."

The closest district office was in Atlanta, but ISB agents spent much of their time traveling to investigate cases all over the country.

She stared at Matt, waiting for him to encourage her to do it, as Chris did. She'd always taken her job seriously, so everyone expected her to be ambitious—and she was, but leaving Natchez wasn't in her plans. Ever.

He shocked her by going in the opposite direction. "You have to do what's right for you, Tory, no matter what anyone else says. Life is about more than a career."

She was grateful that he understood, though she'd often wondered what she'd missed out on by not being willing to relocate. A relationship with the handsome man sitting across from her, for starters.

Was her insistence on remaining in Natchez holding back her life?

Her phone buzzed, and she answered it.

"Tory, we have a call about a disturbance at Pebble Springs Campground," the dispatcher said. "I understand you're back on rotation."

"I am. I'll take it. Thanks, Nina." She stood and pushed away what was left of her meal. "I've got to answer a call about a disturbance at Pebble Springs Campground."

He swallowed his last spoonful of potato salad. "I'll come with you."

"Are you sure? It doesn't have anything to do with your case."

"I don't mind."

She quickly changed into her uniform, then they climbed into her SUV. Her cabin was ten minutes away from the Trace, and traffic was nonexistent. She hurried but was still careful driving down the dark two-lane road. Deer darting across the road were a real hazard, especially at night.

Pulling into the campground, Tory saw a group of partiers huddled around a firepit, where it appeared two men were brawling.

She and Matt jumped in and broke up the fight. From the smell coming off the men and the bottles scattered on the ground, Tory was positive that alcohol had been involved in the dispute. She separated the offenders and instructed everyone to go back to their respective campsites.

Observing how the offenders obeyed her orders, she made the decision not to arrest anyone. No one had been seriously injured, and she could tell that once everyone slept, the situation would mend itself.

Matt was holding one of the brawlers by the arm. "I'm going to make sure he gets back to his own campsite to sleep it off."

"Thanks." She watched the other offender stumble to his RV and climb inside. His wife insisted she would keep an eye on him for the night, and Tory informed the woman that her husband would be arrested if Tory had to return.

As the last of the group dispersed, Tory dictated some notes into her cell phone for the report she'd write later.

She was making her way back to her SUV when she spotted something—an RV that hadn't been parked there the last time they'd come to Pebble Springs.

The tag numbers struck a familiar chord. Kentucky plates. She got out the list that Matt had given her and checked it against the RV.

It matched. The RV had been at the other parks when the murders were committed.

Tory circled the RV and knocked on the door, but no one answered.

She took a photo of the RV and license plate. She would run it as soon as she could to find out who the vehicle belonged to.

At that moment, her phone went off with an alert.

A woman had been abducted at Fort Rosalie.

14

$\mathcal{M}$att's phone dinged with a message. He read the screen, and his gut tightened.

He darted back toward the SUV and spotted Tory walking in that direction as well. "We have to go now," he told her. "There's been an abduction at Fort Rosalie." Fort Rosalie was an old military outpost close to downtown Natchez that overlooked the Mississippi River. The original fort and building were long gone, but the site was national park land despite being in the heart of downtown Natchez. The National Park Service sometimes hosted events there, so Matt suspected something must have been going on that night.

"I got the same message."

While she got them back on the road to downtown Natchez, he read through the entire alert. "Witnesses claim a man shoved a woman into his car and took off. Were they holding an event there tonight?"

"I'm not sure, but there had to be some reason for people to gather there at this time of night. The fort is usually open from sunup to sundown."

The drive seemed to take forever, but once they arrived at Fort Rosalie, there was no denying something bad had happened. Natchez PD cruisers, along with sheriff's office vehicles, lined the area, and Matt could see officers and deputies working in conjunction to talk to witnesses and keep the area secured.

Tory parked her SUV in the middle of it, and they both hopped out. A crowd had gathered along the perimeter, and people were craning their necks in an attempt to catch a glimpse of what was going on. Matt spotted a man in his mid-to-late twenties, an older woman, and a few children, huddled around a Natchez police cruiser. The man was obviously distraught and the woman was doing her best to comfort the kids.

"Matt, Tory, over here," Chris called from where he stood with Chief Scott.

"What happened?" Matt asked as they approached.

Chris consulted his notes. "The family attended a Concert under the Stars event here and were preparing to leave afterward. Twenty-six-year-old Amber Knight and her mother-in-law took the younger kids to the restroom before their drive home. They were on their way to the family's car when a man appeared from behind the building, grabbed Amber, and shoved her into a dark four-door sedan. The mother-in-law screamed for help and the victim's husband came running, but the culprit was gone before he arrived. Other witnesses have confirmed the story. We've placed a BOLO on the vehicle and set up roadblocks around town."

"Could anyone identify this man?"

"Not so far. He was wearing a ball cap and it was dark, so no one got a good look at his face. And by the time Amber screamed, his back was to the witnesses."

Agitation flooded Matt at the notion that they might have missed the murderer once again. If they didn't find that vehicle soon, the serial killer might very well have his next victim.

Matt glanced at the woman's husband, who clutched their kids, his face drawn and haggard. The killer was destroying families, and Matt was tired of always being two steps behind him.

Tory jumped in and helped process the scene. It was the first time they'd had witnesses to an abduction and a crime scene that didn't include a murdered victim. It was a start, but he hated to think what might happen to the abducted woman as they followed procedures.

Video surveillance wasn't much help either. The offender was good at keeping his face hidden, but Matt saw Amber Knight's expression from a security camera that had captured her. She was terrified—and she had a reason to be.

After several hours of questioning, they finally released the witnesses. The chief advised the victim's family to go home and get some rest.

Mr. Knight balked at the idea. "I'm not going anywhere without my wife."

Tory stepped in and took his arm gently. "Care for your kids, Mr. Knight. They're terrified, and they need you to help guide them through this. If we get any information about your wife, we'll contact you immediately. We know where to find you."

He reluctantly acquiesced. "My sister is driving down from Memphis to pick up my mom and the kids. We were here for a vacation. I can't leave without Amber. Please find her."

"We will do everything we can to bring your wife home to you," Tory assured him. She arranged to have an officer escort their car back to the hotel where they were staying.

Matt admired the gentle way Tory had with people. She was kind and soft with crime victims but could be tough as nails when the situation required. He was good with investigations, but his people skills weren't as strong as hers. Another reason to have her on his team.

A police officer approached. "We've got a sighting of an abandoned car that matches the one described by our witnesses."

His heart leaped at the development. He hopped back into the SUV with Tory, and she drove to the site.

They were quiet on the ride to the location they'd been given, both afraid the abduction wouldn't turn out well for Amber Knight.

He spotted police lights off a deserted patch of road. Tory pulled up near the other cars. She'd barely stopped when Matt hopped out and ran toward the vehicle.

Natchez PD already had the dark sedan cordoned off. Both driver's side doors were standing open and the keys were still in the ignition, but there was no sign of anyone near the car.

Matt switched on his flashlight and swept the car. No visible blood.

"Have you checked the trunk?" he asked an officer.

"Yeah. It's empty."

Of course it was. The killer wasn't the type to leave his victim in the trunk. They weren't even on national park property. The killer wasn't going to let a victim go so easily, and he wouldn't be diverted from his established pattern.

"Let's do a search of the area anyway to be sure he didn't dump her somewhere close by." Matt ran a hand over his face, certain it would be a waste of time, but they had to do whatever they could. They were too late. Again. The killer must have had another vehicle waiting and transported Amber Knight into that.

"Did anyone see the suspect or another vehicle here?" Matt asked.

The officer shook his head. "No one saw anything. This area is so deserted that it's doubtful anyone even drove by."

He was right. The road was pitch-dark, with no streetlights, and off the beaten path. There were no houses, no buildings, and no traffic lights, which meant no cameras either. Knight's abductor had specifically chosen the spot to change vehicles—another indication of his meticulous planning. He was toying with them, and that infuriated Matt.

"We ran the car's info, Agent Shepherd," the officer added. "It was stolen hours ago from a business parking lot. The owner wasn't even aware it was missing until we contacted him."

Another dead end.

Officers processed the car for forensics. Law enforcement might get lucky and find the victim's hair or blood inside, but they were merely stockpiling evidence for a potential case against the kidnapper, which wouldn't matter unless they found him.

Deep down, Matt feared Amber Knight's kids would never see their mother alive again.

Because of me. Because I can't do anything to stop this maniac, whoever he is.

He and Tory remained at the scene long into the night, and he could see the toll it was taking on her. After all, she'd gotten out of the hospital the previous day. It was one thing to answer a call to break up a fight at a campground, but it was quite another to spend hours processing a crime scene.

"Why don't you go home and get some rest?" he suggested to her. "I'll finish up here. I'm afraid there's really not much left we can do unless we catch a break and one of the roadblocks comes up with something."

"How can I go home and sleep, knowing what could be happening to that woman?" she demanded, crossing her arms over her chest.

Matt understood her feelings. He'd lived with the same ones for months. "There's nothing else you can do, Tory. All we can do now is wait. And while you wait, you might as well rest so that you're at your best when we can actually do something."

Her voice trembled. "I've got the rangers going over the trails with a fine-tooth comb, but with so many miles of forest, it's unlikely we'll find anything. We don't even have a description of the vehicle Knight must have been transferred to."

She sounded so defeated, and he hated that, but it was part of the job. They couldn't wave a magic wand and find their culprit.

If they could, his job would be superfluous. He rubbed his face. At such times, he would give anything not to be necessary.

There was another reason he wasn't so keen on having Tory at the scene. He stared at a photo the husband had given them of Amber Knight, and Matt couldn't help but notice the resemblance between Tory and the victim. Tory was a few years older, but both women were athletically built and had similar coloring. All of the other victims had blonde or light-colored hair, but Amber Knight had dark shoulder-length hair. She was the first brunette—a change in the victim profile.

If the killer really was getting personal, Matt didn't want Tory in harm's way because of him.

"Natchez PD still has an officer watching your house, don't they?" he asked, trying to sound casual.

Tory rolled her eyes. "Yes. I still think it's unnecessary, but I told him I would call when I plan on returning home."

"Call him. Go home and get some rest. Something tells me we're going to need it tomorrow. I'll catch a ride back with one of the officers."

Still, she hesitated. "Matt, I don't—"

He cut her off firmly. He understood her reluctance, but they were at a standstill. "We're done here, Tory. There's nothing for us to do but wait." And the waiting would be devastating.

Tory took a few steps away from him, then spun back toward him. "I won't leave you, Matt. Not like this." She marched over and wrapped her arms around him, and his instinctively went around her.

He buried his head in her shoulder as the weight of everything hit.

Matt couldn't imagine how difficult it would be to get through the night, and he didn't want to burden her with it too. But being with her, having someone who understood him the way she did—they might make it through together. She finally stepped away and tugged him back to her SUV.

They didn't speak as she drove, and the two-lane road was dark and silent. There were no streetlamps, no stoplights or businesses to break up the darkness. Nothing but their headlights. And it was so quiet that Matt thought they should be able to hear Amber Knight scream, but the lone sounds were the hum of the car's engine, the wind through the open windows, and crickets and frogs.

Tory slowed or stopped frequently to avoid hitting animals—deer mostly—darting across the road. It was too dangerous to speed, so she drove carefully, pulling into each stop along the Trace where their killer might dump his prey.

They drove to Pebble Springs Campground and made the loop, straining their eyes for anything out of the ordinary. Nothing appeared out of place, except for a still-burning firepit which Tory got out and extinguished. There were so many trees, and the summer had been hot and dry. One spark could start a fire that would burn for miles.

They returned to Natchez and then to the sheriff's office, both hoping that once they regained cell service, their phones would pop with alerts that Amber had been found alive and her killer apprehended.

At the sheriff's office, Matt left Tory in the SUV and checked in with the deputy on duty. "Any updates?"

The deputy shook his head grimly. "No sir. Everything has been quiet so far tonight."

Matt glanced at his watch and realized "tonight" had ended hours ago. It was already early morning. He joined Tory once more. "They haven't heard anything."

She didn't seem surprised. "I doubt they will before daylight. Even if the abductor does drop her off somewhere, who will be there to find her before the day starts?"

She was right. They were playing a waiting game with the sun.

"Let's pick up some coffee and head back to my cabin," she suggested. "We can wait it out there as well as here, and it will be more comfortable."

That was a good idea. And perhaps she would get some sleep. The day would be a long one.

Once at her cabin, Matt switched on a police scanner for any updates, as she showered and changed clothes before heading off to bed.

"You'll wake me if you hear something?" she asked, and he assured her that he would. "I could go for a few hours of rest. Maybe you can get in a few winks yourself on the couch."

"Thanks, Tory." They both needed it, but he wasn't sure sleep would come for either. "I'll be fine."

He sat for a while, listening to chatter on the scanner. There was nothing of any real substance. It was a quiet night in Natchez and Adams County.

Finally, he shut off the scanner and hopped into the shower. He didn't have any other clothes so he changed back into the ones he'd been wearing, then flicked on the television and let it play as he sank into the couch. He was asleep before his head hit the cushion.

He had no idea how long he slept, but it was daylight when he awoke to his phone ringing.

He grabbed it from the coffee table and answered the call, his gut already twisting with the news he was certain it held. He was right. The call was brief, and he hung up feeling hollowed out.

He heard Tory's bedroom door open and her on the phone, no doubt getting the same news he had.

He sat up and rubbed his face as she came into the living room.

She looked tired, and her voice was heavy. "I guess you heard. We've got a body." Tears slid down her cheeks.

Before he understood what he was doing, Matt crossed the room and wrapped her in his arms.

She clung to him for several minutes, sobbing quietly, before finally pulling away. "I'd better get ready so we can go."

A short while later, they drove toward the coordinates Chris had given Tory, along the Trace. Matt parked, and they got out. He prayed the crime scene would give them something to work with, but the killer had proven adept at making law enforcement chase their tails.

He watched Tory meet up with Chris to get details. She motioned for Matt to follow her to where the body had been found, behind a marker celebrating some historical event.

Yellow crime scene tape cordoned off a section of land, and Matt spotted the body lying in open grass. As usual, the killer had made no attempt to hide her from being discovered. Matt recognized the victim right away from her photograph, and his heart fell.

Amber Knight.

Her dark hair was spread out on the grass, and a red tube sock was wrapped around her neck. He'd seen the other autopsy reports and knew that wouldn't prove to be the murder weapon. The killer liked to use his hands. But he'd also made certain Amber was marked as one of his victims by including the sock.

"Were there any personal items missing from the body?" Matt checked his notes from the night before. "Her husband said she was wearing a heart-shaped locket." He knelt beside the body but saw no sign of the necklace.

"They haven't found one," Tory said. He could tell she was doing her best to compartmentalize the death, though she was deeply shaken by it. It was too raw. Too fresh.

The offender had ticked off all of his signature boxes. With the dump site, the missing necklace, the strangulation, and the tube sock, there was little doubt it was the work of the serial murderer.

The monster had abducted and murdered a wife and mother, right under Matt's nose.

"There's something else," Tory told him. Her voice cracked, and she swallowed as she took an evidence bag from another ranger and handed it to Matt. "It was beside the body when the victim was found."

The bag held a handwritten note inside the bag. The words written across the slip of paper stopped him cold.

Two down, one to go, Agent Shepherd. Better keep a closer count on your flock.

15

$\mathcal{T}$ory watched Matt's skin pale as he read the note.

More taunts from a killer.

She touched his arm. "We'll find him, Matt. Maybe a piece of evidence we collect today will be the key to locating and arresting him."

He nodded, but she could see he didn't believe her. He'd seen so much during his career, but the current case was affecting him on a different level.

If she was honest, it was affecting her too. Knowing a killer was out there, stalking and murdering women—she shuddered at the thought.

He leaned toward her and spoke in a whisper. "Tory, I don't want you staying alone at your house anymore. I don't think it's safe."

She sighed. *Not this again.* "I'll be fine. Besides, I have the Natchez PD watching my door."

He took her by the arm and pulled her back toward the body. "Tory, I want you to focus, really focus on this woman. Is she familiar to you at all?"

She stared at the victim, her heart broken, but didn't understand what he was getting at. They'd both seen Knight's photo the previous night.

"Tory, she looks like you," Matt said with urgency.

She nearly choked at his insinuation. Sure, they shared a similar physical build and coloring, but they were hardly twins. "I think you're overreacting. Maybe there's some resemblance, but that doesn't mean anything, Matt."

"It does," he insisted. "All of his previous victims had blonde or lighter-colored hair. This is the first victim with dark hair. And, given that he included you in that photo he sent to me—well, I'm not willing to take a chance. He already tried to grab you once, Tory. He's made this personal. I don't want it to get worse."

"What do you want me to do? Quit the investigation?" she asked, incredulous that they were having the circular conversation again.

"No, that won't keep you safe. I want to increase your security."

"Matt, we're searching for a killer," she said. "The rangers are already stretched thin, and so are Natchez PD and the sheriff's office. Without a direct threat, I feel like it's a waste of resources to place a guard on me all the time."

"We don't have to. I'll do it. I'll stay with you and sleep on the couch. If you don't leave my sight, there's no way he can get to you."

She was a little uneasy with the idea of Matt being around her constantly. It was already weird enough working with him, but to have him sleeping on her couch was too much.

But the worry in his expression was more than she could say no to. And it wouldn't be for long. Once they found the killer, Matt would be off on his next assignment and things in her life would get back to normal.

She didn't like it, but he was obviously beside himself with fear for her, and it wouldn't hurt her to be a little more careful. She thought back to how it had felt, seeing herself in that photograph with Matt—another taunt from the killer.

Suddenly, she felt goose bumps rising on her arms as she stared down at Amber Knight. She rubbed her arms despite the Mississippi summer heat.

The killer was still out there, and he had one more victim to kill before he left Natchez and moved on to his next murderous destination.

They had to stop him before that happened.

If Matt had to keep her with him in order to concentrate on capturing the murderer, she wasn't going to stop him.

She nodded her agreement, and he seemed to relax.

Once they finished processing the scene and Amber Knight's body was removed, Tory climbed back into Matt's vehicle. They followed Chief Scott's cruiser to the hotel where Amber's husband and family were staying.

The notification of her death was brutal, and Tory was overcome with deep sympathy for the family who'd sought a simple getaway and would leave forever changed.

But Matt still needed to gather information. "Did your wife mention whether she felt like she was being followed yesterday, before the abduction? Or did you or anyone in your family notice a man following you?"

Mr. Knight shook his head. "No. She didn't say anything of the sort. And I didn't see anyone hanging around."

"I didn't notice anyone watching us either," his mother added.

"We're so very sorry for your loss," Tory told them again, as she and Matt moved to leave. Chief Scott remained behind to discuss further details with the family.

Matt drove to the hotel, and Tory followed him to his room, waiting as he packed up his belongings, checked out, and carried his bags out to the vehicle. Then they headed back to her cabin. Officer Stewart of the Natchez police was already there, waving as they pulled in.

"Do we still have to have my police guard if you're going to be here?" she asked Matt. It didn't make sense to tie up another valuable resource to watch her property when she didn't believe she was actually in any real danger.

John Ricks might not even be their killer. She still didn't understand how he would have found her in the woods and believed it was a coincidence she'd found him there.

She'd made peace with the fact that she might never have an explanation as to why he'd tried to drag her into the woods. Perhaps it had been driven by panic rather than reason. People did all kinds of nonsensical things when they were afraid.

"Let's leave the guard in place for now," Matt said.

The dogs came running as Matt parked. They bounced around with excitement, and Tory stopped to greet each one. She smiled at the sight of Matt crouching to pet Jojo, who ate up the attention, panting and smiling with every scratch under her chin. The other dogs protested by nudging their noses against him, so he petted them too.

Tory smiled. Matt had made himself friends for life.

She walked inside the cabin as he grabbed his bag. Inside, she motioned to her couch. "Make yourself at home, I guess."

He gave her a small smile. "I know you think this isn't necessary, and I promise to be as unintrusive as possible."

Tory didn't see how that would be possible. She wasn't certain her heart could handle his constant presence.

She showered and changed into sweats, then emerged from her bedroom to find Matt at the stove.

"I hope you don't mind," he said. "I made myself at home."

She sat down at the kitchen table and he set a plate of pasta and salad in front of her. "You don't have to cook for me," she protested, even as her stomach rumbled at the appetizing aroma from the food. "It's my home. I should be cooking for you."

"I don't mind," he assured her. "I don't often have the opportunity to cook, and I enjoy it. Besides, it's not like I slaved over the stove for hours. Even I can handle pasta." He twirled some spaghetti around his fork before popping it into his mouth. "Not bad, if I do say so myself."

He was trying to put on a happy face, but she saw the worry creases in his forehead and knew his mind wasn't far from the killer he was hunting. After all, he was there with her because of how personal the search had become.

She set down her fork. "This case is really getting to you, isn't it, Matt?"

His mouth tightened. "When he first contacted me, I thought it would prove helpful, a step that would eventually lead to his capture." Matt blew out a breath and shook his head. "But this—Tory, this is hitting way too close to home." His gaze locked on hers. "I never meant to drag you into it. I shouldn't have. I'm sorry."

"I'm not sorry," she said firmly. "I'm glad you chose me to help you on this case. I'll admit that it was a little unnerving seeing myself in that photograph, since it means a madman is watching us, but I'm not that easy to scare off."

"I wish you were more scared. It might keep you safer."

She reached across the table and touched his hand. "You still see me as the twenty-year-old girl you left behind, but that's not me anymore. I've been through training. I have skills. I've confronted killers and arsonists and bullies. I really can handle myself." She was tired of trying to convince him, but she felt it was necessary. She wasn't the same young woman she'd been when they were young together. She'd grown and changed.

They both had.

He squeezed her hand. "I don't doubt your skills and training, Tory. I've read your file. I am aware that you can take care of yourself. It's just that . . ." He trailed off.

She waited for him to continue. When he didn't, she prompted, "It's just what?"

He took a deep breath. "Being around you again has made me so completely aware of how awful it would be to lose you. I'm terrified at the possibility of something happening to you."

Warmth swept through her, and she laid a hand on his arm. "Nothing is going to happen to me. I'm going to be fine, and we're going to find this murderer. You and I can do anything. Well, almost anything. Remember that bookshelf we tried to build?"

He chuckled and she felt him relax. "'Tried' is the right word. That thing was a disaster. It's a miracle it never toppled over."

She laughed at the memory. It was a good one—of many. "We always had a lot of fun together, didn't we?"

"Yes, we did." They'd been best friends before their relationship had blossomed into more, and she realized how much she'd missed those days, simply hanging out with him.

Suddenly, she was hyperaware that his hand covered hers. A wave of embarrassment washed over her, and she pulled her hand away. His presence was bringing up all kinds of emotions, and she wasn't sure she was ready to go back down that road.

Their lives were still headed in very different directions. Once the case was over, he would return to his life with the FBI, and she would stay in her beloved Natchez.

When it came to their fractured relationship, nothing had changed in fifteen years, and she wasn't sure she could go through that kind of heartbreak again.

She'd barely survived his leaving the first time. How would she survive it again?

She stood and began clearing the plates from the table. "I'll get these cleaned up."

He hopped to his feet. "I'll help."

She filled the sink and washed the dishes by hand. Matt stood beside her, drying each dish as she handed it to him.

Having him there beside her was nice. She'd dreamed a lot about what their life together might have been like if they'd never parted, and it had resembled that exactly—an easy companionship.

She'd dated over the years, but no one had ever compared to Matt. No one had ever set her soul on fire while also making her feel safe, comfortable, and understood. She'd told herself it was because he'd been her first love and she'd romanticized their connection, but as he stood beside her once more, she knew she hadn't exaggerated anything at all.

He hung up the drying towel and reached up to put the plates away in the cabinet. She reached over him to store the glasses and, when her arm brushed his, longing rushed through her.

He slid an arm around her, and before she even realized what was happening, she was wrapped in his embrace, staring up into his familiar brown eyes.

His eyes lowered to her lips, and it was clear that he wanted to kiss her.

She lifted her face to his as he lowered his head, all thoughts of guarding her heart out the window at the right feeling of being in his arms. She would deal with the consequences later.

But the dogs barking outside grabbed their attention.

Tory and Matt sprang apart and scrambled for their weapons. Tory switched on the porch light and threw open the door. Matt was beside her in an instant. There were no new cars in the driveway, so the dogs must have been barking at something else.

"I'll check this way," Matt commented, stepping off the porch and heading to the left while she went right.

She flipped on her flashlight, running the beam over the tree line, but spotted no movement, though the dogs were still barking like crazy.

Matt hurried back to her. "I don't see anyone."

"Me either. Maybe Officer Stewart saw what upset the dogs." She hurried to his vehicle with Matt on her heels.

Tory felt that something was wrong before she reached the car. The door was standing open, and the officer lay on the ground, unmoving. She rushed to feel for his pulse.

"He's alive," she told Matt. "But he's got a gash on the back of his head."

"He was here." Tory didn't have to ask who Matt meant as he yanked out his cell phone and called for backup.

As she waited for the ambulance and Natchez patrol officers to arrive, horrifying comprehension sank in.

Matt was right. Someone had been roaming around her little cabin. Officer Stewart must have seen the perpetrator and tried to stop him.

Someone had been lurking around, trying to get to her house—to get to her. And he was willing to commit violence against a police officer to do it.

16

$\mathscr{M}$att rubbed the back of his neck and watched as the paramedics loaded the injured officer into the back of the ambulance before driving off.

Chief Scott, who'd arrived moments before the ambulance, came toward Matt and Tory. His expression was grim, and Matt felt the same.

"Officer Stewart regained consciousness before they loaded him into the ambulance. He told me what happened. He said he heard noises around the porch, so he got out to check. That's when someone hit him from behind."

"We found him on the ground unconscious," Matt explained. "But we didn't see anyone around the cabin."

"We didn't hear anything until the dogs started barking," Tory explained. "We came right outside and looked around, but we didn't find anyone."

"And neither of you heard anything outside?" Scott asked.

"No," Tory and Matt said in unison.

"What were the two of you doing? Did you have the TV on or something, that you didn't hear anyone outside?"

Matt felt his face flush, but he said evenly, "We were washing dishes when Tory's dogs started barking. That's when we ran out and saw Officer Stewart on the ground. We surveyed the area but didn't see a single soul, or another vehicle."

But they'd missed something. They must have.

Someone had been out there, possibly watching the cabin or waiting for his opportunity to strike. He'd gotten close, and he might have gotten even closer were it not for Tory's dogs and Officer Stewart.

Matt's neck warmed. He'd been too focused on the urge to kiss Tory to be aware of someone lurking in the woods right outside.

He'd let his guard down, and it had put Tory in danger. He couldn't allow his attraction to her to affect his judgment like that again.

He'd joined the FBI to stop monsters from hurting people, but lately it seemed all he did was clean up after the bad guys. He was always one step behind on the case. The criminal had killed multiple women, thumbing his nose at Matt even with so many professionals after him.

Matt had made a mistake in bringing Tory in on the case. He obviously couldn't guard himself from his attraction to her, and if he couldn't keep his wits about him around her, how could he hope to keep her safe?

If he had any chance of keeping her alive, he would have to keep his distance from her, at least emotionally.

Chief Scott arranged a search of the area and woods around Tory's cabin while she and Matt stayed at the house. After an hour or so, the team came up empty. No evidence found that anyone had been there. Except for the knot on the back of Officer Stewart's head.

The killer had gotten way too close.

"I'm assigning a pair of officers to replace Stewart," the chief told Tory and Matt. "They're under strict orders to call in any suspicious activity before investigating—no matter what."

"Thank you, Chief," Tory said.

"We'll find out who did this, Ranger Mills," Scott assured her.

"Tell Officer Stewart I'll be thinking about him," Tory said.

Scott nodded at her, then walked back to his car. In a matter of minutes, all the police cruisers were gone except for two parked at the end of her driveway.

Matt and Tory were alone once again.

"Should we go back inside?" she asked him.

Back inside to where he'd nearly kissed her.

"Maybe we should head to the sheriff's office and touch base with the team. I think I'd like to go back over some details of the case again."

"Okay." She clearly understood that he was no longer comfortable being completely alone with her—and why.

They drove back to the sheriff's office but found that no new information had come through on the BOLOs or the forensics from the crime scenes.

Matt ran his fingers through his hair. Something had to give soon. The killer had already claimed his second victim in the area, and Matt was determined that he would not get a third—especially since Matt had a sickening suspicion that the killer planned on making Tory the next victim.

He had no proof of that beyond his gut feeling, but the killer had made a point of getting close to Matt, getting into his life. His decision to snatch a woman who resembled Tory from a public place in front of so many people had convinced Matt. That was why he'd been so adamant about remaining by her side at all times, but even that had been a mistake.

An email popped up in his inbox, and he opened it.

Finally, the trucking logs from Victor Lance's company. He pulled out his notes listing the dates, times, and locations of each of the previous murders, even though he knew them by heart, and checked the trucking logs against them.

Matt soon realized there wouldn't be much to go on. The logs indicated that Victor Lance had been on the opposite side of the country during all of the murders except the two which had taken place in Natchez.

Matt tossed down his notes in frustration. It no longer mattered that Victor Lance had eluded them at the casino, or that his truck was still being processed. There was no way that Victor Lance could be the serial killer.

Matt yanked Lance's photo off the evidence board he'd created.

"You're removing Lance from the suspect list?" Tory asked from behind him.

"I got his trucking logs. They show that he was nowhere near where the previous murders were committed in other parks."

"So you're certain Lance is not a suspect?"

"I don't see how he could be."

"What about John Ricks?"

Matt leaned against the wall. "I haven't found anything that suggests he was in proximity to our other crime scenes either. I've emailed some of the local agencies to see if he's on their radar, but for now, we have no proof one way or another."

She perched on the table, grimacing at the evidence board. Removing Victor Lance was a necessary step, but it took them backward instead of forward in the investigation. They'd eliminated one of their two suspects, and the other wasn't too promising either.

Matt emailed Vivian to update her on the situation. She'd said she would travel to Natchez to assist, and he hoped she would arrive soon. He could use another set of eyes on the case.

After he hit Send, he grabbed his keys. "I have to go see my dad. Will you be okay here on your own for a while?" He hadn't planned on leaving Tory alone at all, but where could she be safer than at the sheriff's office?

"Sure. I'll be fine."

"You won't go anywhere alone, will you?"

"Where would I go? I'll be here, going back over the case. Don't worry. I'll be fine."

He reluctantly left and climbed into his SUV. He needed to clear his head, and he needed some advice. The best person he could think of to offer it was his dad.

He phoned his father and met him downtown at a diner. The moment his dad slid into a booth across from him, Matt felt better.

His father's hair had grayed, and his walk was slower than Matt remembered it being the last time he'd visited, but Paul Shepherd's powers of observation were still keen. "I can see this case is taking its toll on you."

Matt propped his elbows on the table. "It is. To tell you the truth, the whole job is starting to take its toll. All I see every day is the worst of the worst. I'm not sure I can take it anymore." He was still reeling from the scare with Tory.

"It sounds like you should take a break."

Matt bit his lip. "Actually, I'm not sure a break would be enough. I'm burned out, Dad. I don't know if I can do this job anymore."

He hadn't said the words out loud to anyone, though he'd been thinking them long before he'd taken the serial killer case. Long before he'd come to Natchez and rediscovered what he'd lost all those years ago.

"But I can't stop, at least until Tory is safe. I got her into this. I can't just abandon her now. Plus, I can't let this psycho continue to hurt people. He's made things personal for me. I'm the best one to catch him."

His father reached across the table and placed his hand on Matt's arm. "This is not all on you, son. You're part of a team. No one expects you to solve this alone."

"I believe I can do it," Matt said. "But the cost might be too high."
He couldn't imagine anything happening to Tory because he'd come
to Natchez to hunt a murderer. If he hadn't pulled her into the case,
her life might not be in danger.

"You've always been too ambitious," his dad mused.

"I didn't think there was such a thing as being too ambitious. I
always knew what I wanted and went for it. I didn't think there was
anything wrong with that."

"There isn't." His father studied Matt carefully.

"Perhaps it's because I'm getting older or something, but I'm
starting to realize how much I gave up in doing what I thought I wanted.
Now I'm trapped. I asked for this life, and I can't get out of it. If I quit,
how many people will I let down? What if some other criminal comes
along and does untold damage because I wasn't there to stop him?"

"Son, here's all the advice I can give you. Try to figure out what it
is you really want out of life, and work toward that, like you did when
you decided to join the FBI. Nothing was going to stop you, and you
made it happen. Look at all you've accomplished. Now, it's time to
decide what you want next, and do that again. The FBI will always be
able to keep going. You can't think about what might have been, and
you can't do your best work if you're burned out. The FBI deserves
people who can still do the work, and you deserve a fulfilling life."

Matt sucked in a breath as he realized he didn't have to think hard
about what he wanted more than anything else.

Or rather, who.

He thanked his dad, then stood and hugged him tightly. "Tell
Mom I love her."

"I will. Call your sister."

Matt grinned. "Yes sir."

He watched his father leave, then walked to his SUV.

His dad was right. Matt had always gone after what he wanted with full force. He'd spent years chasing career success and accomplishments, working his way up the FBI ladder. It was time he focused his ambition on what he really wanted.

And it was becoming clearer and clearer that what he truly wanted was Tory.

He'd reached his car and had his hand on the door handle when a voice behind him called, "Agent Shepherd? Agent Shepherd, wait!"

He whirled around to see reporter Chelsea Morrison hurrying in his direction. He braced himself for another request for an interview.

But Chelsea shoved her phone in his face, and he could see that it was recording. "Is it true, Agent Shepherd?" Chelsea asked, winded from running to catch up with him.

"Is what true?"

"I've received a phone call from a man who stated that you're in town to investigate more than one murder. The caller claimed you're in town to hunt down an extremely dangerous serial killer who has already murdered eight women. He called the murderer the National Park Predator." She held her phone right in front of his mouth. "I'm publishing the story in an hour. Care to comment?"

The National Park Predator?

How many people had heard that name?

Only those who'd seen the letters—and the killer himself.

Matt doubted the information had come from anyone on his team or from local law enforcement. In fact, he'd done everything he could to keep that detail from the press, not wanting to flatter the killer by using the name he'd given himself.

That left one explanation. The killer had leaked his own story.

He had apparently decided that if Matt wasn't going to give him the press he desired, he would do it himself.

"Who told you this, Chelsea? Did the caller give a name?"

"It was an anonymous source who was kind enough to also tell me where you were," she replied. "But he sounded very credible. He gave me the names of the other victims and I checked them out. They were all murdered on national park land with the same method. How do you respond to that, and why have you been hiding this information from the public?"

Suddenly, several more people raced in Matt's direction, shouting his name and hurling questions at him about a serial killer in Natchez. A news van screeched to a stop, blocking him and his SUV from the parking lot exit. Someone hopped out, pointed a camera at him, and peppered him with more questions.

Chelsea scowled. She must have thought she was getting an exclusive, but her source had obviously made several calls. From the letters the killer had sent, Matt knew he craved attention and had labeled himself the National Park Predator. Had he decided he'd waited long enough, taken matters into his own hands, and called the press?

Regardless of who'd made the call, the killer was getting the one thing Matt had fought not to give him—notoriety.

*ory tried to occupy her mind after Matt left, but she was still struggling with the fallout of that near kiss, and the new certainty that a killer really was stalking her. If Matt hadn't been there, she didn't know what might have happened.

Then again, if he hadn't been there, she might not have been so distracted either.

Yet she wasn't sorry she'd accepted a place on his team. She'd predicted that it would be awkward and that she would have to guard her heart. It was obvious that the old attraction was still there, but nothing had changed. He was still based too far away and traveled extensively for his job with the FBI, and she still couldn't imagine ever leaving Natchez.

There was no point dwelling on it. She and Matt had far more pressing issues to worry about.

Tory added Amber Knight's crime scene photo to the evidence board. They were still waiting on autopsy and forensics reports. Hopefully, something new would turn up and crack open the case.

There had to be something they were missing.

She decided to go back through the video surveillance they'd collected. Perhaps scanning the footage with fresh eyes would alert her to something they'd overlooked before. She went frame by frame, but nothing new popped out at her. Finally, she gave up. The images had nothing to offer.

A murmur reached her ears from the sheriff's office bullpen. A group of deputies and staff were huddled around a television hanging on the wall. She wondered what they were watching, when she caught a glimpse of someone who resembled Matt on the screen.

Sheriff Ford approached the conference room door and pushed it open. "You need to see this," he stated. His tone was grim.

Tory followed him out of the conference room and into the bullpen. The closer she got to the television, the more she realized how terrible the news would be. It was a video of Matt on the streets of Natchez, surrounded by a group of reporters shoving microphones and video cameras into his face, shouting questions at him.

She heard the term *National Park Predator* and flinched.

Where had they gotten that name?

"Oh no. He hates to be on TV," a voice said behind her.

Tory whirled to see a woman she didn't recognize. The pretty blonde wore nice slacks, a blouse, and a suit jacket—along with a strong air of confidence.

"Can I help you?" Tory asked her.

The blonde's smile didn't quite reach her eyes. She held out her hand to shake Tory's. "Agent Vivian Ferguson, Investigative Services Branch."

The Agent Ferguson with whom Matt had been working. "It's nice to meet you, Agent Ferguson. I'm Law Enforcement Ranger Tory Mills."

Agent Ferguson eyed her up and down. "So you're the Ranger Mills I've heard so much about."

Tory swallowed hard. Had Matt been talking about her? And why was she suddenly dying to hear what he'd said about her?

Vivian chuckled at the discomfort on Tory's face. "I was referring, of course, to Supervisory Ranger Moore. He couldn't stop praising you when I showed up at the ranger station to join the investigation."

Tory felt her cheeks flush.

Vivian gestured to the television. "Matt was doing his best to keep this off the news. I wonder how it got out."

"I doubt the info came from anyone on the task force," Tory mused. "Matt was very clear about what we could release to the public, and no one would dare leak that name."

Vivian nodded and glanced around at the deputies in the room. "I'm sure he was, but it's nearly impossible to keep a secret in a small town like this."

Tory was sure no one in the sheriff's office or Natchez Police Department had spilled the beans to the press, but Vivian was correct. Keeping secrets in a small town was nearly impossible. Even Matt's father had heard about his arrival in town before Matt called him. And the murder of Amber Knight had merely increased the press's interest.

"It is difficult," she agreed. "But I can personally assure you that the law enforcement in this town is professional. None of them would have done this."

Vivian studied her carefully, then said, "I believe you. Either way, it's out there now, and we'll have to address it. Is Matt here?"

"No, he left earlier. I'm not sure when this happened," she said, motioning to the television screen.

Sheriff Ford joined them and addressed Tory. "The mayor called me. When Agent Shepherd returns, we have to put out a statement. I understood why he wanted the case to be confidential, but we can't keep this under wraps any longer. The press knows we're hunting for a serial killer."

Vivian stuck out her hand. "Sheriff, I'm Agent Ferguson of the Investigative Services Branch. I've been working this case with Agent Shepherd. Once he returns, we'll get together with you to work out what we should say as a united law enforcement team. We don't want to cause any further panic."

Ford shook her hand. "Welcome to Natchez, Agent Ferguson."
He turned to Tory. "Come and get me when Shepherd gets back. I'll
be on the phone with Chief Scott."

He walked away and Vivian nudged Tory. "Where are we working?"

Tory led her into the conference room and explained the setup.

Vivian ran a critical gaze over the space. "It's fine. I am curious
about why you allowed Matt to move the task force away from the
ranger station."

"It wasn't my call."

Vivian locked eyes with her. "These murders took place on national
park land, Ranger Mills. They're under our jurisdiction. At this point, we
have more sheriff's deputies involved in the investigation than rangers."

Tory bristled at Vivian's accusatory tone. "The rangers don't have
the manpower or resources to head an investigation like this. We phoned
ISB to take over, and Matt showed up instead. He wanted something
more centrally located, and my supervisor agreed. Priority now is to
stop the serial killer. It doesn't matter who gets him, as long as we stop
him and save lives. Besides, it was agreed that even though the bodies
are being dumped on national park land, they aren't necessarily being
killed there."

"But we haven't uncovered yet where the killer is committing these
murders, despite our efforts. Since the bodies are found on park land,
that gives us jurisdiction," Vivian argued. "We don't want the locals
coming in to contest that jurisdiction."

The agent's words troubled Tory. Vivian gave the impression that
she was more concerned with jurisdiction than with identifying and
stopping the offender.

"We may not know where they were killed, but at least one of
our victims"—she marched over to the evidence board and tapped the
Liddy Martin's photograph—"was abducted from the city of Natchez.

I would say that gives Natchez PD a legitimate reason to be involved in this investigation."

Vivian shrugged. "Then, once we've found the perpetrator, Natchez PD is welcome to file abduction charges, but they'll have to wait in line, because we will be filing federal murder charges first." She scanned the evidence board. "Is this everything you've collected so far?"

"Yes. Amber Knight was found today, so we're still waiting on autopsy and forensics reports."

"What about Liddy Martin's autopsy report? I'd like to see it, along with the rest of the crime scene photos, phone reports, and anything else you have."

"Hasn't Matt kept you up to date on the investigation here?"

"I was wrapping up the last crime scene while working a separate case. He told me what was happening, but I haven't actually seen any of the evidence. I'll need to get caught up quickly. Now that the murderer has claimed victim number two, we're running out of time before he leaves Natchez for good and we have to start all over again."

Tory gathered up the case files and placed them on a table for Vivian to review. It was a lot of reading, and Tory wondered how the agent would get through it all in a reasonable amount of time.

Despite her concerns, Tory was impressed with the ISB agent. Vivian seemed smart and capable, and Tory was anxious to help her get caught up. "Is there anything I can help you with?"

The agent glanced through a file. "I assume Liddy Martin's autopsy report has come in."

Tory found the report and handed it to Vivian. "The autopsy revealed that Martin was manually strangled. The red sock was added postmortem. It wasn't used in the act of killing her."

Vivian scanned through the document and grimaced. "No DNA."

"No, none was recovered. I understand there was some on the other victims?"

"A few of them. Testing has revealed that it originated from the same individual, but he's not in the system. Once we find him, though, we'll be able to tie him to all of the murders."

In the stoop of Vivian's shoulders, Tory saw the same frustration she felt, and that she'd seen in Matt. First, they had to find the killer and stop him.

She rubbed the back of her neck and stared at the evidence board again as Vivian dug through the stack of reports. Maybe the agent would find something they'd missed.

But Vivian, like Matt, had been with the case from the beginning, and they were no closer to identifying the killer.

The conference room door opened, and Matt came in. He looked frazzled and irritated. Tory recalled the scene on the news and couldn't blame him for being in a foul mood. The very thing he'd wanted to keep quiet was all over the press.

"Matt, are you okay?" she asked gently.

He shook his head. "I was basically mobbed by a group of reporters, led by Chelsea Morrison, all demanding information about the National Park Predator."

"We saw." Tory motioned toward the television in the bullpen that was still broadcasting the replay along with the headline, *Breaking News: Serial Killer on the Loose in Natchez.*

His face fell at the sight. "Terrific."

"Sheriff Ford said the mayor is demanding a press conference to try to calm the public. We're supposed to tell him when you're back."

Matt ran a hand over his face. "Okay. I'll take care of it." He glanced behind her to see Vivian getting up from the table where she'd been going through the reports. "Vivian. You made it."

"I got in an hour ago."

"Welcome to the frying pan. Or rather, the fire."

"Thanks," Vivian said dryly. "I can help you coordinate a press conference. I think ISB and Ranger Moore should take the lead on this, Matt. This is a national park case."

"Sure." He appeared unconcerned about her fixation on jurisdiction, but it bothered Tory. The public didn't care who apprehended the killer, as long as he was caught, and Matt had led the case since he'd arrived in town.

"I'll go and speak with the sheriff," Vivian said before leaving the room.

Matt collapsed into a chair. He buried his face in his hands. "This isn't the direction I hoped this case would take."

"I'm sorry Chelsea ambushed you," Tory said.

"That's not your fault. Everything was always going to come out eventually, especially after Amber Knight's murder."

"How do you think the press found out?" Tory asked, recalling Vivian's assumption that someone in law enforcement had leaked the information to the press. She hated to think that was true, but after two murders, she couldn't help but acknowledge the possibility, considering that it was the only one she could think of.

Matt raised his head, his eyes haunted. "I think he called them."

She gaped at him. "The killer? Why would he do that?"

"I told you. He craves control, Tory. He'll enjoy watching the chaos he's created."

Despite the killer's obvious need for attention, it still seemed risky for a criminal who would surely not want to be caught. She shook her head. "There has to be some other explanation. One of the deputies—"

"The killer named himself, Tory."

"I heard. The National Park Predator." That name had stuck with her, and she realized Matt was probably right. "He called himself that in the letters he wrote you, didn't he?"

"He did. And now he's getting everything he wants—the public attention, the fear, all of it."

She followed Matt's gaze to the television, which continued to replay the breaking news. From experience, she knew the press wouldn't let up any time soon. They had a big news story, and there would be no stopping the coverage.

Tory reached for her cell phone and dialed Chelsea's number. She swore she heard smug satisfaction in the other woman's voice when Chelsea picked up. "I hope you're calling to answer some questions now, Ranger Mills."

"Actually, I'm calling to get some answers. Where did you get your information, Chelsea?"

"I can't tell you that and you know it. I don't divulge my sources. However, my reliable source tells me this same serial killer murdered six women in two other national parks prior to coming to Natchez. Can you confirm that, Ranger Mills?"

Tory almost hung up. Chelsea still didn't care about anything but chasing a story. "You do understand that your source was likely the killer himself, don't you? You're giving him the attention he craves. You're enabling a murderer, Chelsea."

"The public has a right to the information that the man who killed Liddy Martin and Amber Knight also killed six other women."

"We were trying not to create a panic. Like the one you've now caused."

Chelsea snorted. "You have a job to do, Tory, and so do I. Now, if you and Agent Shepherd would like to sit down for an exclusive interview, maybe we can work something out. As you might recall, I gave you the opportunity to control this narrative days ago. You refused."

"I'll have to get back to you about that," Tory said, then ended the call before Chelsea could respond. The reporter wasn't going to give up any details about where she'd gotten her intel, but Tory had realized that she might be able to get them another way.

"If it was our serial killer who called Chelsea and the others, I'm sure he didn't deliver the news in person," she told Matt. "If he'd delivered a note or something like that, they would be showing that all over the news, so he must have called them."

Matt's eyes widened. "We can pull Chelsea's phone records and trace the call."

"The killer probably used a burner," Tory admitted, "but it's worth a shot."

"Everything is worth a shot now. He might still be using the burner to keep up with the news. If it's on, we might be able to track it."

They worked together to retrieve phone records while Vivian helped the local police set up a press conference to address the public's concerns.

An hour later, Vivian poked her head into the conference room. "Matt, it's time for the press conference. Let's go."

"You can handle it, Vivian," Matt hedged. Tory remembered what Vivian had said about his dislike of public speaking.

But Vivian wouldn't take no for an answer. "Everyone already knows the FBI is involved. I don't mind taking the lead, but it won't look right if you aren't there too. People will wonder why the guy they're used to seeing isn't involved, and they'll automatically distrust what we're saying. We've set up right outside, and we've already got national news media in town. It'll take half an hour, max. Come on."

Tory peeked through the window and saw that Vivian was correct. News vans from several television and radio stations, many with national feeds, had arrived. It was an impressive feat that so many reporters had made it into town so shortly after the news broke.

Serial killers are probably of high interest to the public, Tory reflected grimly. Matt stood and straightened his tie. "Fine. Tory, I'll be back as soon as I can. Will you keep going through those phone records?"

Tory assured him she would and watched them go, glad she didn't have to participate. She could see Matt didn't want to either. He was more interested in the investigative process than in pandering to the press. Vivian, however, seemed to be within her element. But who was Tory to judge Vivian Ferguson? The ISB agent had worked more cases than Tory had, and she was the expert.

Tory absently listened to the press conference on TV as she continued to go through the phone records. Halfway through the conference, her cell phone rang, and she glanced at the screen with a groan. It was her mother calling. She'd obviously seen the coverage and was either worried that Tory was in danger or angry that she hadn't confided in her. Either way, Tory couldn't deal with the conversation at the moment.

But staring at her phone made her remember the photo of the RV she'd taken at Pebble Springs. She'd forgotten all about it after Amber Knight had been abducted and murdered. Tory pulled it up and jotted down the numbers. With nothing else to do until she heard back about the phone records, she decided it was a good time to run the plates.

She keyed the numbers into the computer and a vehicle registration popped up. It was licensed in Kentucky to a woman named Delores Taylor. If her RV had been present at several of the crime scenes, then she might have witnessed something that could point them to the killer's identity.

Tory searched online for the name and a way to contact her, narrowing by location—and found an obituary for Delores Taylor, dated two months earlier.

She couldn't exactly speak to a dead woman.

Tory found a death certificate and confirmed that the Delores Taylor from the obituary was the same person who'd owned the RV.

But if Delores Taylor was deceased, who had parked her RV at Pebble Springs Campground?

Reading through the obituary for Ms. Taylor, Tory learned that the woman had died in an accident. Tory called the funeral home where the service took place and was able to track down a phone number for Delores Taylor's daughter, Kelly Broussard, hoping to get information about her husband or if she knew who was driving the RV registered in her mother's name.

Tory identified herself, and Kelly Broussard's voice perked up. "Are you one of the rangers investigating my mom's death?"

That threw her off guard. She'd thought Delores Taylor had died in an accident. "I'm actually calling about another matter. I work for the National Park Service along the Natchez Trace Parkway in Mississippi."

"Oh." Disappointment sounded in Kelly's tone. "What can I do for you?"

"I'm investigating an RV registered in your mom's name. If she's deceased, do you have any idea who might be driving the vehicle?"

"Probably her husband, Henry Taylor. They'd been married five years when my mom died, and the rangers at Great Smoky Mountains National Park are investigating him as her possible murderer."

That struck Tory as quite a coincidence. "May I ask what happened to your mother?"

"My mom loved traveling in that RV. When she met Henry, he shared that passion, so they traveled to national parks across the country. One day, I got a call from Henry that my mom had fallen off a cliff. I was immediately suspicious about it. Mom told me that Henry had gotten more and more controlling over the past few years, and she was thinking about leaving him. Then, at the funeral, he behaved as if he were completely unaffected by her death. They'd been married for five years, but he didn't seem to care at all. He acted like taking a few days to appear for the funeral was a waste of his time. The same day we buried her, Henry packed up the RV and was gone again. We haven't seen or heard from him since."

"Why do the rangers believe her death wasn't an accident?"

"They said that area had guardrails that should have prevented her from falling. My mom was always careful. I can't believe this was an accident, Ranger Mills. I know Henry did something to her."

Tory thanked Kelly for speaking with her and ended the call, her mind whirling.

What Kelly had relayed sounded similar to the case Matt told her about. Since Delores Taylor had died on national park land, it was being investigated by the ISB. Tory wouldn't have access to the ISB investigation file, but she managed to locate an incident report and was able to read details the rangers noted before transferring the case.

It was as Kelly Broussard had stated. Henry Taylor claimed his wife was bird-watching and leaned over a cliff to take a picture before stumbling and falling over the side. The rangers had been suspicious of the story, since a guardrail should have prevented her fall. Also, witnesses had heard the couple arguing the night before Delores's death. Yet the report gave no indication of motive, as the financial angle hadn't panned out. As Tory and Matt discussed, there were many possible reasons for one spouse to kill another, money being only one.

And Henry Taylor had traveled to Natchez. What were the odds that he'd been at Great Smoky Mountains National Park when three murders, plus his wife's death, had occurred, and was now in Natchez where two more had happened—and none of the murders had anything to do with him?

Tory pulled up Matt's list again and saw the same RV license number had also been present at Glacier National Park when the first three victims were murdered.

But was there a connection?

She glanced through Matt's list of driver's licenses. Delores Taylor's was present, but not her husband's. There was no Henry Taylor listed in Matt's records. How had Henry managed to get through without having his ID taken down?

Was it an innocent mistake? Or a deliberate act to hide his identity?

Suspected of murdering his wife and allegedly present at all the previous crime scenes, Henry Taylor had become a viable suspect.

Switching to another law enforcement database, Tory entered Henry Taylor's information again. She found a link to his Kentucky driver's license and clicked. If he was hanging around her town, she should be able to recognize him.

Tory's blood went cold as a photo popped up on her screen.

She knew the man, but not as Henry Taylor.

It was Alton Banks, the witness who'd come across Liddy Martin's body in the middle of the Natchez Trace, and who'd been present when John Ricks had attacked Tory and tried to drag her into the woods.

Dread filled her. He was so close. He'd been right under their noses the whole time. Living under a false identity. Playing games with them. Taunting them.

But he had no idea she'd figured out his true identity.

The phone rang and she answered it—the tech lab.

"We were able to trace the number you gave us. It made multiple calls to several different people in the Natchez area this afternoon. You were right. All the calls came from the same number and were made from somewhere in downtown Natchez. However, we aren't able to currently track the phone. The user must have it off. I've placed a trace on it, though, so if it's used again, we'll get a notification."

Tory was disappointed that the lab couldn't track the phone but not really surprised. She thanked the tech, then ended the call. The phone might not even matter anymore, since she'd discovered that Henry Taylor and Alton Banks were one and the same.

She printed off a copy of Henry Taylor's driver's license, as well as a copy of Alton Banks's license. As she stared at the two photographs, she had no doubts.

Alton Banks was Henry Taylor.

And more importantly, he'd been present at each of the crime scenes when the murders had occurred.

Through the window, she saw that the press conference was wrapping up. Vivian was still behind the podium, taking questions, but Matt appeared bored and ready to get back to work.

She dialed his cell phone and watched him through the window as he answered. "Matt, are you done? I need you back in here."

Hope filled his voice. "They were able to trace the phone?"

"No, but I've got something better." She could barely contain her excitement over the discovery. "I found him, Matt. I know who the killer is."

"We're done out here. I'm on my way." He ended the call, tapped Vivian's shoulder, and ducked into the sheriff's office, Vivian on his heels.

The second they stepped into the conference room, Tory rushed to explain how she'd uncovered Henry Taylor's false identity. "I found him, Matt. I found him." Excitement bubbled up in her voice. "It's Alton Banks. Alton Banks is the National Park Predator."

"What? Banks? How?" Matt asked.

"I was checking the vehicle registration on that RV I saw at Pebble Springs the night of Amber Knight's abduction. I noticed that it matched one on your list that was at the last park where one of the murders occurred. But with everything that happened, I never ran the license plate. I did today. The RV is registered to Delores Taylor."

He frowned. "Why do I recognize that name?"

"Delores Taylor?" Vivian echoed. "That's the case I told you about, Matt. The lady who fell over the cliff at the Great Smoky Mountains National Park a couple of months ago. Her husband, Henry Taylor, is considered a suspect in her death."

"Okay. What does that have to do with the serial killer case?" Matt asked.

Tory passed him a photo of a driver's license. "This is Henry Taylor, the man accused of killing Delores."

His eyes widened in surprise. "Alton Banks."

"This is the man who found the first Natchez victim?" Vivian clarified.

"Yes." Tory handed Matt the copy of Alton Banks's license. "We were wondering what motive Delores's husband might have had to kill her. What if she realized that everywhere they went, everywhere they parked, women were getting murdered? Mrs. Taylor might have put the pieces together. It was all too much of a coincidence, so she confronted her husband. That would account for the argument they had the night before she was killed. Henry would have had to get rid of her before she told anyone her suspicion. I called and spoke to Delores Taylor's daughter, Kelly, who said they'd been married for five years and described him as controlling. According to Kelly, Henry Taylor didn't seem particularly bothered by his wife's death either. Instead, he packed up her RV and drove off."

"And when he came here, he inserted himself into our case to keep us off his trail," Matt said.

"Then he did it again when that hiker went missing," Tory added.

"He ensured that he was in your search group, Tory, and he's the one who said Ricks was trying to drag you into the woods. No one else saw that part happen. Is it possible he hit you instead of John Ricks?"

"I glanced down for a second at the license Ricks gave me, and I didn't see the attack coming. That's bothered me since it happened, Matt. Ricks would have had to bend down and pick up the rock, then hit me. There wasn't enough time for that."

"But Alton Banks could have done it from behind you and you wouldn't have seen it. The other witnesses weren't in view of the campsite until after the attack. Their account of the event is that they heard a scream, and when they cleared the tree line, Mr. Banks was standing over you."

Anger burst through her. Alton Banks had tried to abduct her that day. When he'd failed, he'd painted himself as her rescuer.

Vivian patted her shoulder. "This is good work, Tory. Very good work. Now, all we have to do is find this Alton Banks."

Tory was already thinking in that direction. "His RV was parked at the Pebble Springs Campground as of yesterday."

"We need to put out an alert," Matt said. "Call Chief Scott. I'll let the sheriff know and gather a team to find him."

"I'll call Ranger Moore," Vivian offered.

Tory made the call to Chief Scott, then emailed him copies of the two driver's licenses. She gathered her keys as Matt hurried back to her. A sense of urgency had overtaken her since they finally knew who they were looking for and where, as of the day before, he was parked.

"The sheriff is going to put together a team and put out a BOLO on Mr. Banks, but I want to go over and see if he's still parked there," Matt said.

"Hopefully he hasn't yanked up the stakes and left town," Tory said.

"He hasn't," Matt assured her. "He hasn't claimed his third victim yet."

The exhilaration in his expression was contagious. They wouldn't allow Banks to claim that third victim.

"I'll stay here and coordinate," Vivian said as they hurried out.

Tory and Matt hurried to his SUV and raced down the Trace toward Pebble Springs Campground. It would take the sheriff and chief time to put together a team to apprehend the suspect, but Tory agreed with Matt that the best thing they could do was make certain Banks didn't leave the area until they arrived.

Matt pulled into the camp parking lot, and Tory noted that the RV was still in the same spot. "There it is," she said. Her heart rate kicked up a notch at the idea that they were closing in on Banks.

Matt parked his SUV nearby, and they got out. Tory glanced around, spotting several other lots where people had set up. They would have to clear the area before approaching Banks. There was no telling what he would do when Matt and Tory confronted him. He'd already proven he was a madman. Anyone could be in danger if he felt cornered.

But first they had to make sure Banks wasn't inside the RV, waiting to pounce on them.

Tory took out her gun, and Matt did the same. He marched up to the RV and knocked on the door. Tory heard no noise inside.

"Hey, folks," called a man passing by with his wife. "Can I help you with something?"

"Have you seen the man who's parked here?" Tory asked him.

"Not since earlier. He went into the woods with some fishing gear."

"How long ago was that?" Tory asked.

"A few hours."

"Please go back to your campsite," Matt told them, and Tory picked up on the tension in his voice and body. "In fact, I'd advise you to clear out of the area for a while."

"What's happening?" the woman asked nervously.

"Police business. Please go now." Matt lowered his voice to Tory. "I'm going to see about clearing out the area. I don't want any collateral damage when Banks returns."

"I'll poke around inside."

"Good idea." Matt set off down the loop.

Tory heard Matt speaking loudly, followed by the sound of cars and trucks starting up and rolling out of the campsite. She opened the door and stepped inside the RV. She still had her weapon in her hand ready to use if necessary, but it was obvious once she was inside that no one else was present.

Holstering her gun, Tory began to look around. Plants in the window and family pictures still pinned to the wall were Delores Taylor's touch, but the camper was dingy and held a slight odor, as if it hadn't been properly cleaned in a while. The impression was borne out by the coffee cups piled up in the sink.

Maps were spread out on the table. One was for the Natchez Trace Parkway and featured several red circles. Tory scanned the circled areas more closely, realizing that two of them matched the dump sites for Liddy Martin and Amber Knight.

Which meant the third circle was likely where Banks planned to dump his last victim.

A manila envelope tucked into a seat cushion grabbed her attention. She opened it and found news clippings, photographs, and even background information on Matt. Matt had been right that the killer had been trying to make it personal for him. She flipped through the pages and saw biographical information about Matt, including that he'd grown up in Natchez, Mississippi, before joining the FBI academy. She gasped at the extensive data Banks had collected, including photos and addresses of Matt's parents and sister—even his sister's family.

Matt had been justified in worrying about them, and what he'd done to keep them out of the killer's crosshairs hadn't been enough.

Tory opened cabinet doors and dug through the contents. In one, she found a package of red tube socks. The plastic bag was ripped open and a pair was missing from the pack. She had no doubt the lab would be able to match the ones around both victims' necks to that very package.

A tin box on the counter caught her eye, and she moved over to open it, her hands shaking with everything she'd already found. The tin contained jewelry. Amber Knight's heart-shaped necklace rested on top, and it didn't take long for Tory to find the ring taken from Liddy Martin's finger.

If she'd needed any further proof of Alton Banks's involvement, there it was.

Her phone rang and she tugged it out, thinking it must be Matt. Instead, it was her boss. "Tory, what happened? Agent Shepherd is all over the news. I thought he wanted to keep the press out of this."

She struggled to piece together what he was saying due to the spotty reception inside the RV. "He did, Chris, but it doesn't matter anymore. We've identified the serial killer—Alton Banks. Remember the witness who supposedly found Liddy Martin's body? He inserted himself into the investigation from the very beginning."

"Agent Ferguson told me." Chris paused. "Banks? Really?"

"Yes, it's definitely him. I've found evidence in his RV. Matt and I are at Pebble Springs, and people claim he's somewhere out in the woods. We've got a team on the way to bring him in. Do me a favor and make sure the chief brings in a helicopter."

Chris said something that she couldn't make out, and the call dropped. She glanced at her cell and saw she had no service. She hadn't heard Chris's last response, but she hoped he'd heard her request.

Tory realized she didn't even have her radio on her to call in and repeat it. She'd left it behind in her ranger vehicle when she'd hopped into Matt's SUV.

She spotted Matt hurrying back to the RV, and stepped outside to tell him what she'd found.

"I got everyone cleared away from the area," he told her. "Some are moving slow, but hopefully they'll still be gone before Banks comes back."

"Do you think he will return?" Tory asked.

"He should. He doesn't know we're on to him yet."

"Unless he has a police scanner."

"If he has one, he probably doesn't have it on him," Matt said. "And I doubt he'd get coverage out here. Did you see anyone inside?"

"No, but I did find a package of red tube socks with a pair missing, plus a tin full of jewelry. Liddy Martin's ring is in there, and so is Amber Knight's necklace."

"That evidence alone should be enough to tie him to their murders."

She touched his arm. "Matt, there were at least twenty other pieces of jewelry inside that tin."

He frowned and rubbed his chin, the shock of that revelation evident in his expression. "Twenty pieces? We've identified eight victims."

"He must have been doing this for a while before you caught on to him, like you thought. You said you thought he was experienced. Maybe he only recently developed a signature because he wanted the attention."

Alton Banks was in his forties. If he'd been killing since he was a young man, there could have been dozens of other victims they hadn't connected to him yet.

Tory heard the crunch of footsteps and spotted movement coming down the loop. A figure appeared, walking their way. Matt tensed beside her and drew his weapon. She pulled hers too and held her breath as Alton Banks came into view.

He was carrying a large black backpack and fishing rod. He appeared surprised to see them, not because they were there but because they had their guns raised, and she realized Matt had been right. Up to that moment, Banks had no idea they were on to him.

"Freeze, Mr. Banks," Tory commanded. It wasn't the first time he'd seen her, but it was the first time she'd trained her gun on him.

She saw it in his eyes. He knew he was caught.

"I said freeze," she called as he continued approaching, a smirk on his face.

"What's going on?" He glanced around, as if noticing for the first time how empty the campground appeared.

He didn't stop walking.

"I said freeze," she barked again. She wanted answers, but she would shoot him if she had to.

Without warning, he hurled the backpack at Tory, who staggered back, dropping her gun. She scrambled for it, but Banks stomped down on it, his heavy boot narrowly missing her finger. He reached down and scooped it up.

"Don't move, Banks!" Matt shouted.

A gunshot split the air. Matt went down, and Tory screamed.

Alton grabbed her arm and yanked her to her feet as if she weighed nothing. He jammed the gun against her face and dragged her with him up the loop and toward the woods.

Terror mixed with the pain, but she managed to catch a glimpse of Matt, who lay unmoving on the ground as Alton Banks dragged her away.

She finally realized the cold, hard truth. She was going to be victim number three, just as the killer had always intended.

18

*P*ain, then panic. Those were the first sensations Matt felt as consciousness seeped back into his body. He groaned as he forced his eyes open and struggled to focus his vision.

He was on the ground, and his head and side were a wave of agony. He pulled himself into a sitting position, but that made the world tilt sickeningly. He pressed his hand against the ache in his head and rode it out. When he removed his hand, he saw blood.

He'd been shot. Alton Banks had appeared from the woods, shot him, and then taken Tory.

He stumbled to his feet as the realization hit him. He had to go after her.

He pushed through the pain and forced his legs to hold him up, then realized his side hurt too. He gently touched it. More blood. That was the actual bullet wound. Glancing down, he spotted blood on a rock near where he'd been lying on the ground. He must have hit his head on it as he'd fallen.

That made more sense. If he'd taken a bullet to the head, he doubted he would have been able to walk around.

Sirens screamed in the near distance and by the time he'd regained his equilibrium, several police cruisers, vans, and ambulances had roared to a stop in front of him.

Matt held his side as he faced them. He spotted Vivian and Chris Moore exiting a ranger SUV.

"He took Tory!" Matt shouted as they ran toward him.

"Matt, are you okay? You're bleeding," Vivian said.

"Banks shot me, but I'll be fine. We have to go after Tory. He took her." Another round of pain swept through him, and he gasped at the intensity, but he couldn't allow it to stop him. "He grabbed her and dragged her into the woods. We have to go—now, before he harms her."

"We will," Chris assured Matt. "We'll find her, but we have to get you bandaged up."

He helped Matt to a picnic table, where he managed to sit before his legs gave out.

"I need some help here," Chris called, and a man in an EMT outfit hurried their way, carrying a bag of supplies.

Sheriff Ford and Chief Scott approached. "What happened?"

"We found the suspect's RV, but he wasn't around. I cleared out the campsite while Tory searched inside and found a tin of jewelry. His trophies. Banks is definitely our guy. He came around the bend, shot me, then dragged Tory into the woods."

"You've got a good head wound too," the paramedic said as he examined Matt.

"I hit my head when I fell. I was actually shot in the side." He could feel his shirt wet with blood.

"We'll get you fixed up, Agent."

Matt was grateful help had arrived, and even more so to see that everyone had spread out to comb the area. Banks was out in the woods somewhere with Tory, and her life was in very real danger. The thought of losing her when he'd just found her again sickened him. He had to get moving and do whatever he could to find her.

Matt turned to Chris, ignoring the paramedic's protests. "Can we call in a helicopter? Banks was on foot, so he couldn't have gotten very far unless he had another vehicle parked somewhere. I didn't see one pass by, but I don't want to underestimate this guy again. We can use the heat-seeking camera."

Chris nodded. "I'll set it up. Now hold still."

"We've already got teams ready to move into the woods." Chief Scott gestured to the sheriff. "Ford will send his teams east, and we'll go west."

"I've also got a forensics team on their way," Sheriff Ford added. "I'll set someone here to guard the RV as well, in case Banks decides to circle back."

"I can handle that," Vivian spoke up. "And I can start processing the RV."

Matt was glad for their quick responses and teamwork. It left him free to hunt Banks, as soon as the paramedic finished patching him up. Though Matt was grateful, the man was taking entirely too long.

"We should get you to the hospital," the paramedic said.

"No, I'm fine," Matt insisted. He wasn't about to spend hours in a hospital while Tory was out there with Banks. Since he'd been identified, he wouldn't hesitate to kill her. Matt couldn't allow that to happen. He was going to find her, and when he did, he would never leave her side again.

Vivian gripped his shoulder. "Matt, you really should be checked out by a doctor. Your head—"

"Will be fine. It's a little bump." A little bump that made the ground swim, but he could work around that.

"Matt, please. You have to take care of yourself. I don't want to see anything happen to you."

He glared at her. "Vivian, I am not leaving this campground to go to the hospital while Tory is in the hands of a murderer. Don't ask me again."

She must have absorbed how serious he was because she backed off.

He knew how irrational he must seem to her. The last time she'd seen him, he'd been a different Matt Shepherd—one who wasn't in love with a beautiful, intelligent, capable park ranger.

"I'm sorry," Vivian said softly. "I didn't realize how important she was to you."

"No, I'm sorry," he said. "I didn't realize it myself until quite recently."

"Well, this is the best I can do for now, since you won't go to the hospital," the paramedic announced with no small amount of irritation.

"Thanks." He jumped up and hurried to where Moore and Chief Scott were setting up a grid.

Chief Scott handed out photos of Banks, copied from his driver's license, to everyone present. "This is our suspect. He's considered armed and extremely dangerous. He's killed at least eight women, and there are likely more." His jaw tightened. "A lot more. He's abducted one of our own, Ranger Tory Mills. Let's bring her home safely. Radio anything you find."

Matt stared at the photo of Alton Banks and kicked himself for not seeing through his facade sooner. Banks had done everything but walk up and introduce himself as the National Park Predator, and Matt still hadn't seen it. Worse, the killer had placed himself in Tory's path again and again. Banks might not have known about Tory's and Matt's shared past before arriving in Natchez, but he'd definitely set his sights on her early on. If something happened to her, Matt would never forgive himself.

The teams dispersed and began darting into the woods. Matt approached Chris and the chief. "What about the helicopter? Time is not on our side."

"It's on its way," Chris told him.

It would have to do, though everything in him screamed that they didn't have time, that it was Tory's life. Matt scanned the campsite and spotted teams heading toward the trees, blocking roads, and even a crew scouring the RV.

Everyone was doing what they were supposed to, yet he felt as if it wasn't enough to clean up after his colossal mistake. How had he allowed Banks to get the better of him?

The sight of press vans flooding the campsite did nothing to sweeten his mood.

"Keep them back," Matt ordered a group of deputies. "I don't want them near this crime scene."

Chris took a phone call, then said to Matt, "The chopper is about to land. I'll drive you."

Matt followed the ranger to his vehicle. The helicopter couldn't land at Pebble Springs because of the trees and foliage, but the pilot had found a suitable field a mile or so away.

Chris took off down the Trace at top speed. "She's going to be okay," he said aloud, and his tone told Matt the words were more for the ranger's comfort than his. "We'll find her."

"Yes, we will," Matt agreed. He prayed they would make it in time.

He couldn't begin to guess how Banks would respond to being cornered. Matt's profile of the killer told him that Banks had never considered the possibility, that he would always operate as if he were three steps ahead of law enforcement. With his cover blown, would he hold on to Tory, taking the opportunity to torture Matt more than he already had? Or would Banks kill her immediately to make his point, then try to escape Matt and the police closing in on him? He'd be forced to find and use another identity if he managed to escape. At the very least, they'd made that possibility more difficult.

Chris took a sharp turn off the asphalt, and the vehicle bounced along the grassy slope as he went off-road, speeding into a field where a chopper was landing. The rough ride jostled Matt's bullet wound, and he grabbed it, gritting his teeth. He could hardly tolerate it.

Chris brought the vehicle to a halt. "She's tough, Matt. Banks doesn't know what he's gotten himself into. Tory won't go down without a fight."

"Sure." Matt got out and ran toward the helicopter, ignoring the wrenching pain in his side.

The pilot handed him a headset that would protect his ears and enable communication over the loud helicopter. Chris followed Matt with the heat-sensing camera and a case of supplies. He loaded it into the chopper, then returned to his SUV.

Matt watched him go as he climbed into the cargo area of the helicopter, motioning for the pilot to take off.

He was grateful for the encouraging words Chris had offered, but Matt didn't need a pep talk. It was time to get to work and find Tory. He refused to let her go that easily, and he wasn't about to allow Alton Banks to take her from him.

The killer's reign of terror was about to end.

19

*T*ory fought back with all her strength as Alton hauled her into the woods.

Hot tears pressed at her eyes when she remembered the way Matt had lain still on the ground. Banks had shot him, and she had no idea whether he was dead or alive.

But it was only a matter of time before he would take her life. Banks hadn't dragged her out there to let her go—not when she knew he was the serial killer. She'd seen his handiwork up close and personal. If she wanted to survive, she had to get away and flee into the woods. He had her gun, but she was familiar enough with the area that perhaps she could hide out until help arrived.

She tried to yank her arm free once more, but he spun around and punched her in the same place where he'd struck her with a rock, sending her to the ground. While she was down, he hit her again across the face. Pain radiated through her, and the edges of her vision darkened as she struggled to remain conscious.

"That's enough," he growled. He jerked her back to her feet, then flung her over his shoulder and darted through the woods with a speed she wouldn't have believed possible under the extra weight. The motion made her stomach roll, and she floated in and out of consciousness from the pain. She had no idea where she was or how long it had been since she'd come upon Banks at the campsite.

Tory strained to listen but didn't hear any sirens. Did that mean help hadn't arrived yet, or that it was too far away to hear?

When she finally came to, she was sitting against a rock in a clearing. Banks was kneeling at her feet, binding them with duct tape. Her hands had already been bound.

Her head was still pounding from the beating he'd given her. She pulled her hands to her face and gently touched her eye, certain it was bruised and bloody. It was the least of her worries, but it still hurt.

"Why are you doing this, Mr. Banks?" she managed to croak.

She'd thought he was a good citizen, someone trying to be helpful after coming across Liddy Martin's crime scene, but he was a completely different person to her now.

His expression was hard. The other face he'd worn—the kind helper who could navigate the woods and was glad to volunteer whenever he could—had been a mask. She was face-to-face with Banks's true self, the one he kept hidden from everyone but his victims. Matt had profiled that he would be charming and blend in easily, and he had been right. Banks hadn't come off as the monster she would have expected a serial killer to be. He'd used his charm as a weapon against her, and likely against his victims. She'd allowed him to get close enough to harm her several times.

He smirked at her. "Why am I doing this? Why not? I enjoy it, and I'm good at it."

"You killed all those women?" She remembered the victims on Matt's evidence board, and based on the jewelry she'd found in the tin box, there were so many more. "You killed your wife?"

"I didn't want to do that. I preferred the cover Delores provided me. The FBI and ISB were watching for a killer, not a family man traveling with his wife." He shook his head. "But she got suspicious when she realized that everywhere we went, someone died. Then she found some of my trophies and confronted me. I had no choice but to shut her up."

Tory was stunned to hear him confess to killing his wife. She couldn't imagine the kind of life Delores must have lived with the man before her.

And the fact that he was discussing it so openly, so carelessly when Matt's profile said how careful he was, gave her pause. No way he was going to let her live after spilling his secrets. He was a killer, and she was his prey. But if he wanted to tell her everything beforehand, she could make it serve her. The longer she could keep him talking, the better her chances of being rescued. Whether Matt was alive or not, they'd had backup on the way. Chris and the other rangers would arrive to find Matt lying there shot, with her missing, and they would search for her.

"And the other women? Are you sorry you murdered them?"

Banks laughed, sending shivers through her. The man truly was cold as ice. "Sorry? Is a sculptor sorry he sculpted a vase? Is a painter sorry he painted a masterpiece?"

Tory carefully schooled her expression to hide her disgust. "You think you're an artist?"

"I am, and now I'm finally getting my body of work recognized. I've been hunting for a long time, and year after year, I kept expecting to be captured. Finally, I realized how much smarter I was than all these cops and agents. I had to start dumping the bodies where they would be found and leave a signature on them. It was the only way I was going to get the recognition I deserve. They were all too incompetent to uncover my work on their own."

If—when she saw Matt again, she would have to tell him how accurate his profile was. "What sort of recognition? Like on TV? Is that why you called the newspapers and television reporters?"

"Why shouldn't I get the kind of coverage others do? I see those true crime documentaries all the time, but no one ever did a piece on my work. No one ever examined my cases and analyzed me.

Now they will. I mean, how many people do I have to kill before I can get a little news coverage?"

His words held anger and indignation. Matt had used the lack of news coverage as leverage, doing his best to ensure that Banks didn't get the publicity he wanted so badly.

"I want my story to be written up. Books, documentaries, TV specials. That's what I want, and that's what your famous boyfriend can give me. The Black Creek Killer made his name, but soon your agent will be known for far more. 'National Park Predator eludes the FBI again.'"

He was already writing his own press. *Disgusting.*

"But you'll still be in prison," she pointed out.

He waved away that notion. "They have to catch me first."

"Now that they have your name—"

"I'll change it. Banks isn't my real name, and neither was Taylor. I'll become someone else again. It's not that hard. Maybe John Roberts or Robert Johnson. And sure you can recognize my face now, but there are ways around that too, for someone as clever as I am." He grinned at her as if he were having fun with his game, rather than being hunted down by law enforcement for his heinous crimes.

But as distasteful as his bragging was, she had no doubt it was keeping her alive, so she had to endure as much of it as possible. "Why do you tie a red tube sock around their necks? I've seen the autopsy reports. You don't use it to strangle them. Why do you add it afterward?"

It must have some sort of significance. He didn't have to do it, but he had with each of his victims—at least the ones they knew about. Was it simply a way for him to mark a murder as one of his?

His expression darkened. "There was a girl in high school with me. She played on the soccer team, and she wore these tall red socks."

She must have played an unwitting role in his deviant development. Had she rejected him? Laughed at him? Humiliated him to the point where he felt that he was getting back at her with every woman he killed? Not that she held any real fault in his offenses. Banks was responsible for all those deaths. Banks and no one else.

"What did she do to you?" Tory asked, clinging to her knowledge that he longed to talk about it all.

He snarled. "I had a crush on her, and she thought it was funny. She used to laugh at me. After a particularly humiliating incident, I started daydreaming about wrapping my hands around her neck and choking the life out of her. Then, one day, I actually did it. I liked it. But even after I'd killed her, I could still hear the laughing. Killing other women like her made it stop, so I kept at it. No one would ever laugh at me again."

"Weren't you afraid of getting caught?" Tory asked.

"Sure, at first. I was waiting to be captured, sure the police were always right around the corner—until I realized they weren't. I was so good at covering my tracks that I wasn't on anyone's radar. I was glad, but as the years passed and I saw other people like me getting all the attention, I grew envious. I wanted that too. Killing became less about taking revenge for the laughter and more about getting the recognition I deserved. I'd been ignored for so long that I would have to do something to make sure the cops would find the bodies. I thought including the red sock would make it impossible for them to ignore. It was riskier, but I'm finally getting some attention. That's worth it to me. And of course getting your famous boyfriend involved has been icing on the cake. If I got his attention, plenty more would follow."

He tore another piece of duct tape from the roll, double-checked that her feet were secure, then walked away, sliding the tape into his backpack.

Matt had been right when he'd said the killer had made things personal. Banks was trying to get his fifteen minutes of fame, and he'd hitched his wagon to Matt's FBI career to make it happen.

Matt.

Tears welled in her eyes.

Was he alive? Would she ever see him again? Would she ever get the opportunity to tell him how much she'd grown to love him again?

Not as long as she was tied up there. She would be another footnote in the story of a serial killer, another piece in Banks's sick portfolio.

Another photograph for Matt's evidence board.

She swallowed hard at that thought.

She'd seen evil in Banks's eyes and knew what he was capable of. Her pleas wouldn't matter because he didn't care about anything except himself and his legacy of work.

She had to make a decision. She could either keep Banks talking and pray that someone found them in time to rescue her, or she could try to escape into the woods while he was distracted.

It wasn't a hard decision. She didn't want to be remembered as another of his victims.

He'd taken her gun from her during their initial struggle, but she always kept a small pocket knife tucked inside her boot. If she could reach it, she might be able to cut herself free before her captor realized it. She was lucky that he hadn't thought to search her for any other weapons.

Banks had his back to her as he dug through his pack, probably taking stock of his supplies. She doubted he'd planned on going on the run so soon. No matter what he told her, they'd surprised him back at the campsite.

She had to move while he was distracted. She slid her hand down to her boot, then dug inside until her fingers curled around the pocketknife she kept there.

Slowly, she tugged it out and opened it, keeping her eyes on Banks. It was a small knife that would probably do little for self-defense, but it was sharp and would sever her bonds, given enough time. He was still oblivious as she dug the tip of the knife into the duct tape at her feet and started sawing at it. Banks had wrapped it tightly around her feet several times, so it would take some time to get through.

She prayed he wouldn't turn around.

Relief rushed through her as the last bit of adhesive gave way. At least with her feet unbound, she could run. She dug the knife into the tape surrounding her hands and started cutting at it, the angle awkward. If she could free them, she would stand a better chance of fighting him off if she had to.

She stared at her gun in his pocket. Ideally, she would retrieve her weapon and take him down, but one thing at a time. She dug into the duct tape with renewed determination.

Finally it yielded, and her hands were free.

If she could reach her gun, she could end the nightmare.

She scooped up a handful of loose dirt and rocks from the ground before climbing silently to her feet. If she could surprise him, she might stand a chance of getting out alive.

Suddenly, Banks spun around.

She hurled the dirt into his face, then lunged for him as he clutched his face and stumbled backward, howling. The gun fell from his pocket, and he rolled on top of it.

Her best hope was to run and pray he didn't catch up to her.

She took off into the woods, as he shouted after her. She wished she could have retrieved her gun, but that would have been too risky with him on top of it. It would have put her within his reach, where he could have overpowered her. She had to put some distance between them—fast.

If he caught her again, there would be no escaping a second time.

She pushed through the brush and high grass, aware that she was leaving a trail, but it simply couldn't be helped. Stealth was less important than covering ground at the moment.

Pausing to catch her breath, Tory strained to hear the sounds of the parkway, but there was no traffic noise. She had no idea where she was or which way it was to the road, and she had to find some way back to civilization. She must find a way to let Chris and the other officers know that she was still alive.

She imagined a search party was already out to find her and Banks. They must have found Matt by then, since they'd requested the sheriff ready a team. But were they even working in the right place? She had no idea how long she'd been unconscious, but Banks couldn't have gotten very far away on foot, could he? But then why didn't she hear any sirens, voices, or movement?

All she heard were the sounds of nature and the pounding of her own heartbeat.

Movement in the trees grabbed her attention. It must be Banks catching up with her. She ducked back into the brush and kept running. Eventually, she would have to find someone or something that could orient her surroundings. Once she knew where she was on the nature preserve, she could find her way to help.

She ran without stopping for a while, but eventually, her legs began to grow weak and her breathing heavy. Her head spun, and she felt sick. His first attack on her hadn't completely healed, and the subsequent blows weren't making the situation any better.

Tory couldn't keep up her pace much longer, but she had to try, if it meant saving her life.

She was thankful for the covering the woods gave her, but still aware of the trail she was unintentionally blazing. She'd traipsed over grass that wasn't used to being walked over by anything but wildlife and, in her haste to escape, she couldn't cover her tracks very well. Anyone could probably track her—and Banks wasn't just anyone. He'd said it himself. He'd been hunting for years.

He would eventually find her.

He had the skills to survive off the land. She did too, but without a gun, it wasn't a fair match. He would easily find and overpower her.

She stopped to catch her breath again and prayed she could find something that would give her some bearings. She couldn't hear much over the wheezing of her breath and the thump of her pulse in her ears.

Tory realized suddenly that it wasn't the pounding of her heart she'd heard.

She spotted a chopper flying low overhead.

She took off running again, following the chopper as best she could. She broke through the trees and into a clearing, where she could see it circling the area. She screamed and waved her arms, doing her best to be seen by the passengers aboard.

She spotted movement above, and then the chopper banked back her way.

Her heart soared, and tears streamed down her face.

They'd seen her. They were coming to rescue her.

The helicopter hovered above the clearing and lowered a bit, and Tory spotted someone hanging out of the cargo area.

Matt was alive and had come to find her.

The pilot circled overhead, but even Tory could see there wasn't enough room in the clearing for him to land the chopper.

She wanted to scream at them to hurry, but it wouldn't do any good. If the pilot couldn't land there, they could send her location to the others, and someone would come to rescue her.

Hopefully before Banks found her.

There was so much she wanted to tell Matt, so much she wanted to say to him. She'd been crazy to push him away, crazy to let him leave town without her, and she wanted him to know it. She wanted to tell him that she would be with him no matter what their futures held.

But her sentiments remained behind her lips because there was no way he would hear any of them over the helicopter blades.

"I'm coming down, Tory," he shouted, and she could see him clicking ropes together.

The pilot lowered the chopper as far as he could, and Tory ran toward the trees so she would be out of the way of the propeller blades. The pilot needed all the space he could get.

She held her breath as Matt slid down the ropes. She didn't breathe again until his feet hit the ground.

He disconnected himself from the ropes, then waved to the pilot, who lifted the helicopter away from the clearing.

The nightmare was finally over, and she never wanted to be separated from him again.

But the smile on his face vanished. He reached out to her, despite the distance that remained between them. "Tory, watch out!"

Hands grabbed her from behind, and the blade of a knife pressed against her neck.

Alton Banks's hot breath rolled over her face as he sneered at her. "You'll never escape me, Tory," he hissed as he dragged her back into the woods.

20

$\mathcal{M}$att gave a shout and sprinted toward where Banks and Tory had disappeared into the tree line.

His heart was racing at the idea that he'd come so close to saving her, only to let that madman get his hands on her again.

He drew his gun as he ran. He had to stop Banks once and for all.

Matt darted into the brush and spotted Banks, holding Tory at knifepoint. Her face was colorless and filled with terror, and he spotted droplets of blood beginning to form beneath the blade. With a flick of his hand, Banks could end her life before Matt even had a chance to take a shot.

"Stay back," Banks warned him.

Matt aimed his gun at the man even as fear rattled through him. He couldn't lose Tory before he got the chance to tell her how hard he'd fallen for her again. He wanted a future with her. Marriage, kids, growing old together—all of it. But Matt couldn't show the maniac what taking her life would do to him. Banks would simply act out of spite.

Who was he kidding? Banks knew. That was why Tory made such a compelling victim for him.

Matt had to take the shot and put the serial killer down for good, but fear pelted him. Fear of hitting Tory. He couldn't imagine his life without her, and he didn't think he could live with himself if he was the one who removed her from his life permanently. But Banks wasn't going to let her go either. He'd been exposed, and he wasn't going to go quietly.

"Let her go, Banks," Matt ordered.

Tory cringed as Banks pressed the knife deeper into her throat. She whimpered a little, but Matt could see she was trying to be strong. Matt gripped his gun tighter and swallowed hard. Things would get ugly. There was no way around it.

"This is it, Matt. We finally meet," Banks said. "What do you think? Was I a worthy adversary?"

"You're just another criminal I intend to get off the streets, Banks."

He shook his head and flashed Matt a smug smile. "I'm more than that. I'll make your career. I'll make us both famous."

"That's not going to happen."

"They'll write books about me. I'll finally get all the recognition that I deserve. You went through my RV, right? You found the trophies. You comprehend that there are many more bodies out there, don't you?"

Matt had already determined that the offender was angling for validation through the media. It was the reason Matt had done his best to keep the details of the case from hitting the papers. He hadn't wanted the press to give the killer a name that bolstered his ego, and he'd mostly been successful in that. But watching Banks, Matt realized he'd merely been delaying the inevitable. The National Park Predator would get his name recognition after all.

"This will be my final triumph, Matt. I'm finally going to get the acclaim I deserve."

"Not if you kill her," Matt said, an idea blooming in his mind. "If you kill her, I'll bury you and your story. No one will ever hear about you. The name Taylor or Banks or whatever your real name is will be lost forever. I'll make sure of it." He meant it. His determination must have been visible in his expression, because Banks let a hint of worry show on his face.

"Let me go," Tory said to Banks, her voice hoarse with fear and pain. "If you let Matt take you in, you'll get your story. You'll get the recognition you want. There'll be jailhouse interviews and documentaries about all the women you killed." Her breath caught, but Matt could see her words were reaching the murderer. "You'll be famous."

Banks lowered the knife as if considering her words. He was clearly torn between his compulsion to control his own legacy and the reluctance to go to jail.

Matt held his breath and waited. He had seen that Tory was persuasive, but was she really about to talk Banks into surrendering?

The killer had lowered the blade, though he still had his arm around her neck. He was actually considering her offer. But a second later, he sneered, and Matt knew the killer had rejected it. He wasn't going to surrender. He wasn't going to jail. Banks cared more about his life than his legacy.

Matt locked eyes with Banks as rage filled the murderer's expression. He raised the knife and plunged it into Tory's shoulder.

Tory screamed, and Matt saw his whole world falling apart. Nothing would be right without her, and he couldn't allow the killer to take her life.

But even through her pain, Tory obviously kept her wits about her. She collapsed against Banks's arm, forcing him to drop her—giving Matt a clear shot.

He fired, and kept firing until Banks fell.

Matt moved toward him, keeping his gun trained on Banks until he found the knife the man had used and kicked it out of reach. Matt searched Banks for any other weapons but didn't find any.

Rolling the killer over, Matt saw no signs of life. He checked for a pulse, then holstered his gun.

The National Park Predator was dead.

Matt rushed to Tory. She pressed her hand against her shoulder, and blood blossomed through her shirt and spread on the ground around her. She was losing too much too fast.

"Stay with me," he said, slipping off his jacket and pressing it against her wound to stop the bleeding. He reached into his pocket for his cell phone, thankful when he got a signal. He called Chris. "I've got Tory, but we need help," Matt told Chris when he picked up.

"The pilot relayed your location," Chris replied. "We're on our way now. Is everything okay? Where's Banks?"

"He's dead, but he stabbed Tory, and she's losing a lot of blood."

"We'll be there in a few minutes."

Ending the call, Matt sat on the ground and gently eased Tory into his arms. All the color had drained from her face, and she was barely conscious. He patted her cheeks. "Stay with me, Tory. Don't you leave me."

She was getting paler by the second, and the blood flow hadn't slowed much. Help had to come at once, or she was going to fade away from him.

He touched her face, murmuring to her. He couldn't lose her again, knowing that the loss would be permanent. "You hang on."

"Did—did you get him?" She struggled to put words together. She was going into shock from the loss of blood.

"Yes, I got him. He can't hurt anyone else."

She gave him a faint smile, but her eyelids fluttered. "Good."

A fresh wave of fear swept through him. He tapped her cheeks again to grab her attention. "Tory, stay with me. Do you hear me? Don't you leave me."

She gave a faint smile and rested her head against his arm. "I'm not the one who left, Matt," she reminded him, and he couldn't help but laugh that she was bringing that up at such a time. It had to mean that she was going to be okay if she could still manage to push his buttons.

He clutched her close and whispered in her ear. "Never again, Tory. I love you. I'll never leave you again."

Her body went limp, and Matt was afraid he'd never hear her say it back.

What was taking help so long to arrive?

He knew they were way off the road and it would take time, but time was something she didn't have. Finding two small people in the woods would not be an easy task, even with knowledge of the general area where they were located. Matt could get up and go find them, but he couldn't bring himself to leave Tory.

He touched her face once more, praying he didn't ever have to say goodbye to her again.

Finally, he heard the roar of ATVs approaching. "We're over here!" he bellowed, straining to be heard over the engines.

"I see them," someone called.

"Please help her," he shouted, his voice cracking with desperation as several deputies pulled up around him.

"What happened to her?" one of them asked.

"Banks stabbed her in the shoulder."

A paramedic lifted the bloody jacket Matt had used to stanch the bleeding and examined the wound. "Help me get her into an ATV so we can take her to the helicopter," he ordered two deputies. "We have to airlift her to the hospital right now."

Matt didn't want to let her go, but he did. She had to get medical aid immediately. Airlifting her to the nearest trauma center was her best chance at survival.

Chris ran up and helped Matt to his feet. "I want to go with Tory," he proclaimed, ready to argue if necessary.

But Chris didn't challenge him. "I'll help you over there."

Seeing her strapped to a gurney and losing blood fast had drained him. The confrontation with Banks had nearly done him in, especially with his own injuries.

Chief Scott approached. "You shot the killer?"

Matt lifted his chin. "He had a knife to Tory's neck, then he stabbed her. I had no choice but to shoot."

"We'll take care of cleaning this up," he assured Matt. "You go take care of her and get some medical attention yourself. I'll get a full report from you later."

Matt climbed onto the ATV and rode to the helicopter. He helped load Tory in for the flight to the hospital. The paramedics boarded and started working on her, inserting an IV and placing an oxygen mask over her face, then doing what they could to stop the bleeding.

Matt climbed aboard too and found a spot beside her. As they rose into the air, he reached down and took her hand, squeezing it gently.

Tory's eyes fluttered open, and her gaze found him.

He pasted on a smile for her. "You're going to be okay. We're taking you to the hospital."

She reached for the oxygen mask the paramedic had placed on her, and Matt placed a hand over hers to stop her. "Keep this on, honey."

She ignored him and tugged it down. "I have to tell you something, Matt. It's important."

"It can wait."

She shook her head. "No, it can't. It's already been too long."

He couldn't begin to guess at what could be so important that she would forgo oxygen to tell him, but he knew her well enough to know she wouldn't rest until he listened to her. "What is it?"

"I love you."

His heart full, Matt leaned over her and kissed her lips before placing the oxygen mask back over her face. "I love you too, Tory," he told her, the words cementing his life's direction for good.

It had taken him fifteen years to find his way back to Natchez, to Tory.

He wouldn't waste another minute.

21

$\mathscr{A}$gent Vivian Ferguson was all over the local and national news, discussing the case of the National Park Predator.

As she watched the TV from the comfort of her couch, Tory cringed that they were using that name, and she saw Matt grimace as he stood behind Agent Ferguson while she gave a press conference to announce how they'd solved the case, identified the killer, and taken him out. He'd fought so hard not to use the name Banks had given himself.

Tory found the press conference amusing, especially since Ferguson hadn't even arrived in Natchez until the case was nearly finished. Matt and the FBI should be the ones celebrated, not the ISB and Agent Ferguson.

But Tory was a little biased on that matter.

Jojo, Bingo, and Bob darted from their spots on the couch and ran to the front door, barking and whining.

Tory switched off the TV, pushed back her blanket, and carefully rose from the couch to see what their commotion was all about. A National Park Service SUV pulled into her driveway, and Chris got out. She opened the front door of her cabin, and the dogs bolted past her down the porch steps to greet her boss.

Chris reached down to pet each dog before approaching Tory. "How's the shoulder?"

Her arm was still in a sling, but she was on the mend. It stung slightly when she moved it wrong, but it wasn't bad, all things considered.

She'd been lucky Banks had gone for her shoulder instead of her throat, or she wouldn't be alive at all. "It's okay. I'll be back to normal in a few weeks."

"That's good to hear."

She wondered what had brought him there. He'd tell her in his own time, so she slid into one of the rockers on the porch.

Chris took the other. "Listen, Tory, I wanted to let you know about something. I got a notification today that there's an opening for a new agent in the Investigative Services Branch. I think you should consider applying for the position. You would be great at it, and now that you've got this momentum going from helping to bring down a serial killer, you're a shoo-in for the job."

She was still flying high from the recognition she'd gotten for her involvement in the case. It had been good experience, and had opened her eyes to a lot of things—including how evil one person could be. She shuddered to remember the fear Alton Banks had sown in her.

But that wasn't the most important thing she'd taken from the traumatic course of events. She'd learned a lot more than investigative procedures and profiling skills. She'd learned how important it was to hold on to the dearest things in her life.

"I appreciate the confidence you have in me, Chris, but I love my job and my home. I'm not interested in moving." Although she had spent some time considering what she was willing to give up to be with Matt. She'd promised herself that they would be together no matter the cost, although they really hadn't talked about how their future might work out. He'd been so busy for the past week, tying up the details of the case, that she'd barely seen him.

Chris stood, obviously unsurprised by her decision. "I had to mention it. I think you could do great things there, and it would certainly be good for your career."

"Are you trying to push me out? Do you not want to work with me anymore?" She'd meant it as a joke, but his expression grew serious.

"No, Tory, that's not it. It's the opposite. I think you're an excellent ranger, and I would hate to lose you. But you would make a great criminal investigator, and you would make more of an impact in that role. Most people want to move up in their careers, and few of us will ever get the opportunity you have now."

"I'm sorry. I don't mean to be flippant," she said, meaning it. "I'm thankful for the chance, but if this experience has taught me anything, it's that life is about more than ambition. I'm happy here. I can't imagine leaving my home."

At least, not for a job. She didn't say that part out loud, but she was seriously considering what it would take to pull her away from Natchez.

The dogs started barking again as a dark SUV parked next to Chris's in her driveway. Her boss grinned at her as Matt climbed out. "Maybe there'll be another reason for you to consider moving."

She stood and gave Chris a playful one-armed shove off the porch as her face warmed with embarrassment. He knew her too well.

"I'll call and check on you tomorrow." Chris shook Matt's hand as he passed, then climbed into his SUV and left.

Matt stepped up onto her porch and produced a bouquet of flowers he'd kept hidden behind his back.

Tory accepted them, breathing in the lovely scent. "Thank you, Matt. They're beautiful."

"So are you." He leaned down to kiss her.

She soaked in the feeling of him, and how loved and protected she felt in his presence. Tears sprang to her eyes at the thought of his whispered words when she'd been hurt. He hadn't repeated them since, and she couldn't even say for certain whether or not she'd imagined his declaration of love.

Things had shifted in the week since that awful day when they'd confronted Alton Banks. They'd finally reached the end of the case, and she faced the too-real possibility that Matt would leave her again to return to his life and career at Quantico.

But was she willing to give up everything to be with him? Or could her heart bear to say goodbye to the man she loved—again?

She sat back down in the rocker, and he slid into the other. "How is the case wrapping up?"

"Good. We gathered all the trophies from Alton's RV and are able to tie him to the eight murders we know he committed. We're still trying to discover who the others belong to, but there will be others. I believed him when he said he'd been killing for a long while before he came across my radar."

Tory shuddered. She'd believed him too. "And don't forget about his wife. He confessed to killing her."

"Delores wasn't tied to the other murders because she didn't fit the profile we'd established, and he didn't use his signature with her. She was older, she wasn't strangled, and her body wasn't dumped. Her death might have fallen through the cracks if it weren't for you, Tory."

She was glad that Kelly Broussard would finally have the truth about her mother's death. It wouldn't bring her back, but it would provide some closure for her and the rest of Delores's family.

"Victor Lance—the guy witnesses saw fleeing from Liddy Martin's crime scene—finally surfaced. He'd been on a drug binge and had no idea he was the subject of a manhunt until he contacted his wife and she told him the FBI had been searching for him. Gambling wasn't his only addiction."

"I feel sorry for his wife and children."

"Me too. Maybe Lance will finally get the help he needs. Oh, and John Ricks was apprehended by New Orleans police this morning.

He's being held on multiple outstanding warrants. I doubt we'll file any charges for the attack against you. With Banks as the sole witness to what happened, I'm more inclined to believe he was the one who attacked you instead of Ricks. Especially since it happened so quickly."

"I agree." She shuddered again, recalling the feeling of his breath on her neck as he enjoyed the terror his threats elicited from her. "So everything is wrapping up. Does this mean you'll be leaving Natchez soon?"

Tory hated to think about it, but the distance between them was an obstacle they couldn't seem to overcome. She couldn't imagine leaving her cabin or her hometown, and he had a flourishing career. What he did was so important.

"For a little while."

Her mind snagged on the words. "What do you mean?"

"I've made a decision, Tory. I'm retiring from the FBI. It's not what I want any longer."

"What?" She was stunned. She thought he loved his job with the FBI. "But, Matt, you've worked so hard to get where you are."

"I have, but it's not what I want to do anymore. I have a new dream, new goals."

She realized the possibilities his decision opened up. "What are you going to do now?" She held her breath as she waited for his answer, feeling as if they stood on a precipice, and his next words would determine whether they fell or flew.

"I'm going to write that book the publisher has been asking for. I might consult on cases on the side, but it'll be at my discretion." He reached for her hand. "I can do all of that from right here in Natchez, where I'm supposed to be."

Tears filled her eyes. "You—you're staying in Natchez?"

A smile spread across his face as he nodded. He stood and pulled her to her feet, holding her hands. "I am. I've made my decision, Tory.

I don't ever want to be without you again." He stroked her cheek. "I've lived too long without you by my side. This whole experience has made it crystal clear that what I want most in life is you. Whatever I have to do to make that happen, I'll do it. I'll never let anything separate us again. Will you marry me?"

Her heart was racing. He was saying everything she'd dreamed of hearing. He was offering everything she'd ever wanted—the love of her life, plus the home she treasured.

"Of course I'll marry you, Matt. I love you so much."

He wrapped his arms around her and kissed her.

And for the first time in her life, Tory was truly home.